The Mission

By

TOM ASWELL

1

It was such an embarrassing campaign that I was relieved to be leaving this planet. Four months in space might give me a chance to clear my head and dismiss thoughts of the nastiest campaign since the 1992 race when Lee Atwater pilloried Willie Horton in order to destroy Michael Dukakis and elect George H.W. Bush.

It was the most divisive presidential election since 1860. More divisive even than the 2000 election in my estimation. But now, despite all odds that it would not, *could not* happen, a lunatic fringe demagogue had been chosen to lead the country only because voters detested his opponent more.

His name was Andrus Blount. It was a tainted election at that. Allison Rutledge, his opponent, had come off as cold and calculating to voters. Her insincerity was surpassed only by her shrillness and quick temper. There wasn't a member of her campaign entourage who had not felt the sting of her wrath at least once. More than that, she had colluded with the hierarchy of her party to undermine populist Senator Mica Kavanaugh's efforts to secure the party's nomination. Emails leaked to the press clearly showed that Rutledge and the party chairman had conspired to wrest the nomination from Kavanaugh, a voice of reason in a wilderness of political rhetoric who had been mounting a strong campaign against Rutledge.

But all that was insignificant in comparison to the actual campaign for POTUS once she had the nomination firmly in hand. The personal attacks, filled with vitriolic rhetoric from both camps only served to fuel voters' distaste for politics, a distaste already saturated by the seeming inability of Congress to govern because of an inexplicable loyalty to party over the welfare of the nation.

Blount, a billionaire businessman who somehow managed to lose the popular vote by nearly six million votes while winning the key electoral vote, appealed to a base that was at once resentful of and largely dependent upon, the largess of the federal government. The irony was lost on the bloc that elected him that Blount was against raising the minimum wage which would adversely affect more than seventy-five percent of his supporters who were hourly employees. It never registered that his opposition to tighter OSHA regulations would directly affect their own safety at work. It never occurred to the vast majority of those who voted for him also hunted and fished, and that his opposition to environmental laws would impact their favorite pastimes—and their overall health—negatively.

The only issue of substance to the largely uneducated, unsophisticated majority who put him in office was his overt opposition to illegal immigration and his manic fear-mongering about Islamic and Hispanic citizens that recalled the days of McCarthyism. And of course, his less-than subtle racial inferences only served to stoke the fires even more.

Now, more than three years into his term, there were half-a-dozen investigations underway. The investigations ranged from Blount's claim of voter fraud that prevented him from an even bigger majority, interference in the election by foreign governments, and Blount's own involvement in conspiring with those same foreign powers to win the presidency. There were even formal investigations into his private business dealings with foreign governments.

For his part, Blount immediately set about further galvanizing his base by antagonizing once close allies in Europe and Asia. America was still reeling from the acrimonious campaign that carried over into the first months of the new presidency and the seeds of real concern about Blount's mental stability were beginning to take root.

Blount was exhibiting with each passing day what the majority of the electorate had known: that he was ill-prepared for the job and more and more, was proving to be mentally imbalanced as well. It became immediately evident that race-baiting was his mantra, a cue to the hate groups like the KKK and the Nazis to go on anti-black, anti-Semitic, anti-Hispanic, anti-Islam and anti-everything-else attacks across the American landscape against anything that did not conform to his vision of greatness, i.e. Anglo Saxon.

Seemingly intent on inducing domestic strife even further, he also began cutting programs designed to benefit the poor, the elderly, and the mentally disabled. As he ridiculed each of those in various public forums, he quickly set about pushing for programs to abolish all social programs, slash corporate taxes while leaving the burden to the middle class and the lower income. He dismantled all programs that addressed environmental issues and pulled funding for the arts and for the education of Native-Americans. Even as he did so, he boasted that he had created millions of jobs, an outrageous lie in and of itself, especially given his brief time in office.

Turning to international affairs, he insulted heads of state, threatened to pull out of important multi-national treaties—and then did so—and rattled swords at the rest of the world intimidating allies in general and threatening hostile nations in particular, pushing the nation to the brink of nuclear conflict.

And woe be unto any reporter who asked the wrong question or challenged Blount on any of his outrageous claims. The so-called mainstream media, even before his election, was quickly elevated to become his prime target. His most strident criticism was the coverage of first his campaign and then of his administration. Even so, he proved himself adept, even in his deteriorated mental state, at diverting attention from his diplomatic blunders, outrageous statements, twitter messages and a myriad of lawsuits pending against his business empire. As if he were somehow orchestrating the media, his boorish behavior invariably pushed the bigger news of the day off the front pages. He had hijacked the daily news cycle. Moreover, his behavior only whetted the appetite of his supporters for more of the same. They couldn't get enough of him.

As if all that were not enough, there were rumblings, distant at first but then growing in number and volume, that he might actually attempt a bloodless coup of sorts by cancelling the presidential election now a little more than three years away on the dubious grounds of national emergency, real or imagined, in effect setting himself up as some sort of supreme dictator. The most disturbing element of that report, while still only a rumor, was that his support base, small though it was but inexplicably propped up by the intolerant and incoherent, largely Protestant religious right, nevertheless solidly—and incredulously—supported such a move. It instantly drew comparisons to such tyrants of history as Hitler, Stalin and Idi Amin. Paradoxically, it did nothing to dissuade his adoring supporters as they became louder and shriller with each passing rally. Blount's handlers orchestrated these rallies ever-so-carefully, screening crowds so that only his hysterical, rabid boosters' voices could be heard over those of the smattering of protestors on the nightly newscasts.

As all this was playing out, other forces were at work to ensure that his image as savior of the cause remained firmly intact. One arch-conservative entrepreneur, a communications tycoon, began snapping up radio stations throughout the country consolidating them into a single mega-network that dwarfed all conservative predecessor networks. Blount even launched his own television "news" network which began airing news stories skewed by his interpretation of what the events of the day meant. The trajectory of his nascent presidency was unprecedented in American history.

And Americans were more divided that ever before. The Civil War was a mere blip on the radar screen of divisive politics. The entire country was in a state of mass hysteria with half dreading the next utterance from Blount's mouth and the other half celebrating it as validation of their own warped sense of values and justification for their fears and prejudices.

Meanwhile, insanity ruled the day as the world moved ever-closer to nuclear carnage every time Blount spoke or tweeted some inane message to his followers. The media, drunk on its own perverse system of values that had long before abandoned the principles of real journalism, hung onto every tweet, every word, every nuance as if the world's future depended on Blount's next observation on anything from movie actresses to race relations to nuclear weapons, complete with misspellings and grammar that were revealing in their own right.

andrusblount@Verified account@POTUS.com: *Tallentless actresses think they know about running a country than me. Sad. I know more about acting than they do.*

andrusblount@Verified account@POTUS.com: *We have*

8

nukes and I'm not afraid to use them. Towelheads need to know that.

His arrogance was boundless.

As quickly as he could offend one-time diplomatic allies and foes alike, members of his party, desperate for his approval and willing to do anything to avoid a public berating by Blount, put up a united front in his defense in Congress. There were exceptions, men of the unique courage to stand up against his excesses. They were quickly put in their place by a flurry of withering tweets designed to solidify his core of supporters who, in reality, counted for only about thirty-five percent of the voting public. But they were a vocal thirty-five percent and the voices of reason were easily drowned out by them.

When race riots broke out, Blount was there to champion the cause of the white supremacist thugs and to admonish the peaceful protestors. When there were mass shootings, as were becoming more and more common in a country obsessed with military weaponry, he, like the others in Congress who were bought and paid for by gun manufacturers, said it was not the time to discuss the control of high-powered semi-automatic weapons. It was never the time. And when a disaster like raging forest fires destroyed hundreds of homes and millions of acres of land or when a hurricane devastated the nation's Gulf Coast, Blount was agonizingly slow in his reactions, preferring instead to tweet about whatever or whoever had most recently offended him.

andrusblount@Verified account@POTUS.com: *good aim. That's the only gun control I care about.*

andrusblount@Verified account@POTUS.com: *people who build where hurricanes floods and fires hit should not expect government bail-outs. But my administration doing more than anyone in history to give relieve.*

His bludgeoning style of governing was driving the wedge dividing the country ever deeper as the top wage earners, those Wall Street barons, drug company CEOs and the contemporaries at the big oil companies and military hardware manufacturers got ever-richer while the rest of the country continued to live from paycheck to paycheck—and some not even that well.

It was also a menu for certain disaster and the pot was already beginning to simmer in middle class suburbia, on college campuses and in the work place, as well as in the slums where distrust of government and resentment toward both parties was palpable. Rumblings of discontent and disenchantment were beginning, quietly at first, because one is reluctant to be the first to complain. But as parents stared at increasing college tuitions for their kids, as stagflation crippled earning and buying power, as costs of medicine, consumer goods and housing continued to climb and as Washington became less and less sympathetic even as the nation's infrastructure continued to crumble, the rumbling grew louder. But Blount couldn't—or wouldn't—hear and neither did his party members in the House and Senate. They had collectively become inured to the rapidly declining state of affairs.

This was the mood that existed as Sol Orbiter One's team prepared for their mission. There was little wonder that the nation, given the current climate, was in a mood to give scant attention to seven people about to blast into space for a trip around the sun.

But you can see why we were damned sure ready for our little getaway.

2

In addition to his racist attitudes, homophobia, Islamophobia, simplistic solutions to complex issues, and overall boorishness, Andrus Blount was now the world's most prominent misogynist. That was revealed during the campaign when a tape of a conversation between Blount and a golfing buddy was released.

One of the members of Blount's foursome, a golfer known only as Jim, had alertly turned on his cellphone recorder when he realized the subject of the conversation. He later had a major contractual dispute with then-private citizen Blount. But when he became candidate Blount he gave a copy to CNN. The CNN version was heavily redacted because of the language but was posted in its entirety on YouTube and the message lost no clarity.

"Marriage is an institution created solely by women for the advancement of the female agenda," he was heard saying. "Marriage is by women, about women, and most of all, *for* women. If that weren't true, bridesmaids would wear matching blue jean cutoffs and halter tops. Men are so stupid they don't know what real happiness is until they get married and then it's too late. The only reason women want men around is because a vibrator can't mow the lawn. But they still need a vibrator so they can have sex with someone they love."

His golfing buddies erupted in laughter, which only encouraged him to go on.

"This whole thing – the male-female relationship and the institution of marriage – is part of a pattern that's existed since the dawn of civilization. Men have to have sex, or at least they think they do, so they fall into the trap that's not really that elaborate and it's a trap set by an

11

inferior intellect. But because of that abundant, talentless commodity called nooky, men continue to fall into the trap. Men are addicted to sex and women are nature's drug dealers.

"American women, while generally incompetent at life, still deem themselves superior to men because men must get the abundant, talentless commodity they married for," Blount continued, uninterrupted other than by laughter from his audience. "That's why I've never married an American woman. And that's why you should remember three fundamental rules: never sleep with anyone crazier than yourself, never sleep with a woman who has more troubles than you, and never argue with a woman when she's tired – or rested. If American men were not so dimwitted and clueless, American women would be living in homeless shelters."

"Women treat sex as the ultimate prize and reward. In reality, it's an act without any skills at all. It's treated so special by women because they know it is the only thing they're willing to give – or capable of giving. That's why they grow stale so quickly. Jim, no matter how beautiful a woman may be, some man is tired of having sex with her, tired of putting up with her crap. Why else would a man would enter into a monopolistic relationship – marriage – with monopoly pricing for an abundant, talentless commodity?"

"Love is the triumph of imagination over intelligence, the delusion that one woman differs from another. I'm not being hard on women; I'm being objective and realistic – and I'm right."

When those lurid comments were publicized widely in the media just before the election, he dismissed it as "macho braggadocio."

Despite his seeming contempt for American women, Blount won the election, thanks to the turnout of the so-called evangelical Christians, the so-called champions of family values.

3

We went about our tasks efficiently and without conversation, the tension during our final preparations was palatable. Silence settled over the room as we, seven astronauts hand-picked for this mission went about our individual check lists in the hours prior to the Sol Orbiter One's scheduled lift off.

The mission had been scrubbed twice already. Once it was inclement weather that delayed the launch. More disconcerting to us was the leak discovered in a valve that put the second launch off for more than two weeks. But now all systems were go and the reality of what lay ahead occupied the thoughts of each of us.

In a matter of a few hours, we would be hurled into space where we would attain record speeds never before imagined for a manned spacecraft on a journey equally unimaginable. It would make the 1969 moon landing by Neil Armstrong and company look like child's play, no disrespect to the Apollo Eleven crew.

In its boldest mission ever, NASA had quietly approved a mission to orbit the sun on the same orbit path as Earth's—but in the opposite direction. The goal was to determine the ability for manned missions to expand even further into unprecedented depths of space at speeds never before attempted. We were the guinea pigs.

NASA's goal was to have Sol Orbiter One travel more than halfway around the sun before its rendezvous with Earth. The Earth's orbit around the sun is almost ninety-three million miles and the Earth travels through space at a speed of sixty-seven thousand miles per hour.

The speed needed for a rocket to escape Earth's gravitational pull is eighteen thousand miles per hour and one hundred forty-four thousand miles per hour to escape the sun's gravitational pull. Because there was no need to escape the sun's gravitational pull, NASA scientists had agreed to push the envelope to the edge of that number and to have Sol Orbiter One travel at a speed just under that rate, one hundred forty thousand miles per hours, far in excess of NASA's fastest previous speed of just under twenty-five thousand miles per hour but a snail's pace compared to the one hundred eighty-six thousand miles *per second* speed of light.

Of course, even a sudden thrust of twenty-five thousand miles per hour would be lethal to a manned crew. The speed would be reached gradually and then only after the craft was free of the Earth's gravitational pull. As top speed is attained, crew members feel virtually nothing once in space. By traveling at more than five and one-half times the previous top speed and at just more than twice the speed of Earth, Sol Orbiter One was calculated to travel a little more than two-thirds the way around the sun before linking up with Earth slightly more than four months into the mission. Sol Orbiter One would, if all went according to plan, travel slightly less than sixty-three million miles to Earth's distance of just more than thirty million miles. If, as I said, all went according to plan.

News of the mission was met with a collective yawn by most Americans, long accustomed to space missions that were once such a novelty but now so routine as to hardly be considered newsworthy. We were non-stories. NASA personnel and scientists, of course, were the exceptions, along with amateur astronomers scattered around the country. The nation's indifference was partly due to the fact that the country had just come through the most contentious presidential election campaign in our history. The brewing turmoil left little opportunity for the country to collectively pause long enough to devote more than passing attention to the Sol Orbiter One mission.

But all this was far from the minds of all at NASA, including those of us who were members of the seven-member crew, some of whom would be going into space on this historic mission for the first time. There was no way to allow distractions, especially as emotional as politics, to enter our minds at such an important time as this.

It wasn't as though we didn't have opinions, of course; each one of us certainly did. Three of us, after all, had voted for Blount. But even those three were privately having second thoughts. I was one of them.

It was against this backdrop then, that NASA and the Sol Orbiter One crew under my command prepared for the greatest space adventure in the agency's history. Each Sol Orbiter One crew member was acutely aware of the importance of not becoming embroiled in partisan debate. The only partisan subject not off-limits was the friendly banter of whether Alabama, Ohio State or Southern Cal stood the best to be college football's national champion for the upcoming season. But even that exchange was limited to Wilhite, Booth, Vasquez, and me—to the exclusion of the other three who knew little and cared even less about football.

4

It was a crew selected as much for its compatibility as for its skill. And I'd be lying if I said it was not deliberately diverse in its make-up. Of course, skill was critical but being able to work together was just as important. After all, if we were going to be spending four months together in a tiny capsule orbiting the sun with no radio contact with Earth for most of that time. As a team, we were put through endless tests of endurance, both physical and emotional and team members were kept in proximity to one another for extended periods in their training in order to ascertain their ability to not only work together and tolerate each other, but to build upon the kind camaraderie that lets each one know that every other member of the team can be counted on when confronted with a crisis.

The training was a process of elimination as well as a course of training and preparation. In a span of more than three years, eighteen candidates had washed out and now, at long last, the team was complete. It was comprised of two women and five men, an African-American, two Asian-Americans, one Hispanic, two Caucasians, and a Jew.

****

My name is Travis Whitten. I am career Army with the rank of colonel and the only African-American chosen for the Sol Orbiter One mission and I was lucky enough to be named as the flight commander. Make no mistake, though, I worked for it and prepared myself for this assignment my entire life. I earned it. My responsibilities are for the overall mission success and for the safety of the crew and shuttle. As the title implied, I was in command of Sol Orbiter One during launch and through the actual descent back on Earth four months after launch.

I'm thirty-seven years of age. I spent my childhood in rural northeast Louisiana's Delta farm country. If you've never been there, it's poor country. And it's flat. My dad used to say it was so flat, you could look out across the Delta and see the back of your head. He was a high school principal and Baptist minister and under his tutelage, I eschewed sports in favor of books as much because of my slight build as for a thirst for knowledge. I'm living proof that a black kid doesn't have to excel in athletics to escape poverty. Now that adulthood and physical training have given me the general physique of an athlete, I'm too old and too disinterested in sports other than a devoted spectator with season tickets right behind the Astros' third-base dugout. I once appeared headed for my father's alma mater, predominantly black Grambling State University upon graduation from high school. But when the original appointee to the U.S. Military Academy at West Point opted for LSU and frat parties instead, I received a belated though no less welcome appointment from my congressman.

My father was Levi Whitten. He grew up picking cotton but worked hard and became an educator and minister. Under his wise counsel, I concentrated on the more difficult high school and pre-college mathematics courses—trigonometry, advanced algebra and calculus—and sciences, especially physics and biology. I was my high school valedictorian but I was shy as a kid. I mumbled my way through my valedictory speech. Because of a combination of all these factors, I had no other option than to be serious about my studies. Thanks to my dad, I had the discipline to ease my entry to life at West Point. I plunged into my academic work, rarely taking advantage of the town liberty given plebes each Saturday from noon to midnight. Not to pin any bouquets on me, but my dedication paid off when I graduated third in my class.

It carried over into my career. I was fortunate enough to be in the right places at the right time and I moved up the ranks rather quickly, I guess. Like I said, the physical regimen of the academy also enabled me to add hard muscle tone to what had been a rather slight frame. Attached to the Pentagon, I managed to pursue an advanced degree in mathematics from Georgetown University, taking as many night courses as my schedule reasonably permitted.

As fate often intervenes, so it did when I met Phoebe Travers in one of my classes. She was from South Carolina. We were married after dating for two years—Those two years were an eternity to me because I was in love, but she still says it more closely resembled a whirlwind romance to her. Truth is, I proposed on our fourth date and kept it up until she finally relented. I still think I just wore down her resolve out of sheer persistence. Back home in North Louisiana, on our increasingly rare visits, no one seemed to even notice—and certainly no one ever mentioned—that she was white. We live in Houston with our three beautiful children.

****

Damon Wilhite, fifty-two, a retired Air Force lieutenant colonel from Brookhaven, Mississippi, was selected as my pilot for the mission. A graduate of the Air Force Academy, he had been an All-Mountain West Conference defensive back. He was a veteran of two previous shuttle flights and was considered one of NASA's top pilots after eleven years with the program. Likewise a resident of Houston (in truth, we all live there), he was married and the father of four children. His oldest son, himself a graduate of the Air Force Academy and like his father, a pilot, had already served two tours in the Middle East though he was never really sold on the war's justification and objectives.

Lieutenant Colonel Wilhite, in a prepared and pre-approved statement, said of the upcoming mission, "This will be the biggest challenge any astronaut has ever faced. I consider it a privilege to have been chosen to work with this crew. The greatest test of nerves will be the complete radio blackout when we lose contact with Earth. That will be a time of true deep space silence. The only communication we will have for nearly four months will be with each other. We'll be completely on our own during that time but I have full confidence in the carefully-chosen members of our crew."

****

Dr. Hubballi Patel will be the physician on the mission. His responsibilities, as his title might infer, was to ensure the crew members remained in good health and good spirits on the lengthy voyage.

18

He would have to be alert for the first symptoms of any ailment among the crew because, in such an enclosed environment, any malady would spread quickly and pose a real and dangerous threat to the crew's ability to function. Such an occurrence could quickly prove catastrophic, so for that reason, his medicine bag was fully equipped with antibiotics and steroids, as well as the usual supply of treatments for motion sickness, diarrhea, and nausea. Unfortunately, he had nothing for boredom which is always a problem. In addition to the crew's general health, Dr. Patel would also serve as nutritionist and exercise guru for the crew. Nutritionist was a job less important that one might expect, given that the variety of food and drink aboard a space shuttle was extremely limited. Exercise leader was another matter. Crew members would be required to stick to a tight regimen in order to maintain muscle mass and to overcome the loss of bone density, a common occurrence on extended space flights.

A graduate of UCLA, the forty-five-year-old doctor attended Harvard Medical School and was a staff physician at Johns Hopkins in Baltimore before joining NASA. Both his parents had immigrated to the U.S. from India in the nineteen fifties when they themselves were but children. Though Dr. Patel and his wife, Sympura, nine years younger than he, were practicing Hindus, that was the only remnant of India to which they still clung. Both were long since fully Americanized as second generation Indian-Americans. Both their children, a girl and a boy, ages eight and eleven, respectively, were home-schooled by Sympura. The boy, Benjamin, had been a National Spelling Bee semi-finalist a year earlier, but lost when he failed to spell *appoggiatura* correctly..

****

Sarah Bergmann was Jewish and a scientist who would be responsible for logging data into the shuttle's on-board computer for analysis upon returning to Earth. She would observe the effects of shuttle life on the rest of the team throughout the mission. Chosen for her analytical detachment, she was as close to robotic in her work ethic as any human could be. Unemotional, straightforward to the point of bluntness, and largely devoid of social skills, she was often considered aloof, even rude, by those who didn't know her. But her six crew mates knew better. We had, after all, spent many months with her in training for the mission and we knew she could let her hair down in a relaxed, non-working environment. We also knew we could rely on her for accurate, unvarnished truth in everything she said, a character trait we each understood and appreciated.

Raised in an upper middle-class family in Brooklyn, Sarah, forty-three, mirrored the manner in which her family had always approached matters, both big and small. Only after considering all sides of an argument or situation, were decisions made in the Bergmann household. Her parents passed those deliberative attributes on to Sarah and her brother and sister just as both sets of grandparents, survivors of Hitler's Holocaust, had passed them to their children. A graduate of Columbia University, Sarah had never had a serious relationship, much less given marriage a second thought. She was perfectly content to lose herself in her vocation. Rumors, which she steadfastly refused to acknowledge or repudiate, held that she was gay. Her crew mates could not have cared less; we placed greater importance on her professional abilities, which were impeccable.

****

Nguyen Huy, forty-two, was born in America a little more than a year after his parents fled South Vietnam just prior to the 1975 fall of Saigon. His parents, once settled in Florida, refused to accept assistance from any American governmental agency. His father had been a police chief in Saigon and became a skilled auto mechanic. His mother had worked at the U.S. Embassy in Saigon before the family was among the last refugees airlifted by helicopter off the embassy rooftop as the communists closed in. She ran a seamstress shop. With their meager income, they managed to send six children, including Huy, through college.

Nguyen attended public schools in Navarre Beach, Florida, and graduated at the top of her high school class. Her valedictorian address, *The American Dream: Born on a Saigon Rooftop*, went viral on YouTube. Offered no fewer than fifty-three academic scholarships from around the country, she chose to remain at home and attended Florida State University where she majored in computer science. She moved on first to the University of Maryland for her master's and then to the University of Washington in Seattle where she obtained her doctorate and immediately went to work of Microsoft. Recruited by NASA, she moved to hot and humid Houston after three years in rainy Seattle. Nguyen did not actively pursue a career as an astronaut and in fact, never applied. She was chosen as a crew member on the basis of her acumen in mastering complex computer programs.

Nguyen was married to a Thai who earned his livelihood in a more conventional way as a sales representative for a pharmaceutical company. They'd been married for sixteen years and her parents, who had wanted her to marry one of her own, a Vietnamese, only now were accepting him into their family unconditionally. At least, they reasoned, he wasn't white. They were yet to come to terms with her decision to allow herself to be blasted into space. This mission was to be her first and hopefully, her last. She did not like flying. But at least there would be no TSA lines to endure.

****

Rafael Vasquez, twenty-eight, was the youngest member of the Sol Orbiter One's crew. A mechanical engineer, he would have the critical job of keeping the shuttle's non-electrical systems operative. Those included everything from the suction pumps for the toilets to the compressors for oxygen flow and temperature controls—in short, everything mechanical vital to keeping the crew alive during their eight months in space.

Vasquez had probably the most interesting biography of all the crew members. He grew up in the El Paso barrio where his father worked as a janitor and his mother was a domestic worker. He was excluded from most of the amenities enjoyed by those from the white neighborhoods. But rather than festering in bottled-up resentment, he applied himself to making sure he would escape the constraints of his youth. Baseball was the only diversion he allowed himself to pursue while attending a mostly Hispanic public high school. A slick-fielding shortstop with a fair amount of pop in his bat, he was good enough to be offered a partial scholarship to the University of Texas-El Paso. But because NCAA rules limit collegiate baseball programs to only partial scholarships and because he knew an engineering degree would be too rigorous to allow time for baseball, he instead jumped at the opportunity to accept an aid-based, full academic scholarship to Texas A&M.

Upon graduation, he entered the U.S. Army as a second lieutenant and married a beautiful registered nurse, Rosalita Ramirez, who also worked as a part-time TV model for a Houston automobile dealership. They had a son, age three, who was already displaying encouraging signs of his own engineering ability with his Lego building blocks. Now a captain, and only five years into what he hoped would be an Army career, Vasquez's goal was to retire in his mid-forties after twenty more years. He was hopeful that while still in his prime working years, he could go to work as a civilian engineer at one of the petro-chemical plants that dotted the landscape between Houston and Lake Charles.

****

Daryl Booth, thirty-six, a native of Omaha, Nebraska, was the electrical engineer on the mission and responsible for all electrical operational systems. While the crew depended upon the skills of Whitten, Wilhite, and Dr. Patel, Vasquez and Booth were the low-profile crew members who would hold our entire mission together. Other than Pilot Wilhite, Booth's job was the most complex on the ship. In the event of an electrical failure, we all could freeze to death in minutes. In the unlikely event that we might survive the temperature plunge, the loss of a fresh oxygen supply would certainly be just as fatal. And just as fast. Of course, only with a dependable electrical system could the computers and navigational equipment function. A failure could hurdle the Sol Orbiter One off course instantly and plunge the shuttle either into infinite space or into the sun itself. Neither option was considered optimal.

Booth attended the University of Nebraska where he excelled as an electrical engineering student and as a pretty fair tenor in the university's men's choral group. He met his wife, Denise, when they were cast members of the university theater's production of *Othello*. They were married two years later and now had four children.

His hobby was collecting vintage Volkswagens. He owned two classic beetles, a nineteen fifty-one and a nineteen fifty-eight, three Karmann Ghias, an antique Volkswagen pickup truck and two nineteen fifties-era Volkswagen buses, all fully restored and in perfect running condition. Once, while dancing with Denise at a party, he whispered in her ear that she was "as easy to steer as a Volkswagen," a remark that,

22

considering his passion for the classic cars, she correctly took as a compliment.

The folks at NASA had picked a good crew. Of course, I had veto power over all selections. Truth be known, I did, in fact, exercise that power on several occasions. The reasons varied and I don't care to go into them. But finally, these were the six people I settled on to get us all back home alive in four months.

5

Andrus Blount was furious to the point of hurling ketchup at the dining room wall.

Waiting outside the Oval Office, Senate Leader Mike Stevens and House Speaker Doug Winstrom could hear his tirade through the closed door to the Oval Office.

The White House staff had seen him angry before and the silent code to stay out of his way was quickly picked up by butlers, cooks, guides, interns, military aides, and upper level flunkies. Still, this time seemed different, more intense. Doors were being slammed, which was not unusual in itself. But never had he slammed a door only to re-open it just so he could slam it again. Ash trays, plates and cups were being heaved across the Oval Office as Blount today more resembled a petulant child than the leader of the free world.

It was when his encrypted cell phone crashed against the door that Chief of Staff Liz "Dragon Lady" Lawson had heard enough. Bursting through the door, she shouted, "Mr. President, that's enough!" She was one of the few people in the world who could speak to him that way. Defiantly, she stood with her arms crossed in front the red-faced POTUS. "You can't continue reacting this way every time you hear something you don't like," she said.

"I can't help it," he muttered. "Have you seen what they're doing to my foundation?"

"Yes, everyone's seen it," she said. "It's all over *The Washington Post*, *The New York Times*, *The Philadelphia Enquirer*, CNN, ABC, CBS, NBC. Did you think they'd all just ignore something this important?"

25

Lawson was talking about the federal investigation of the Blount Foundation which had just that morning culminated in the shutdown of the foundation after prosecutors had determined that Blount used it for personal financial gain for himself and his family. The foundation was only part of a much larger investigation into Blount's financial empire that included massive real estate ventures and a bogus university ostensibly established to help entrepreneurs start their own real estate ventures but which in reality was nothing more than a sham operation designed to separate students from their life savings.

Blount was fuming and barely heard Lawson as she continued. "You cannot afford to react publicly to this because you were supposed to have divested yourself from your business interests when you became president…"

"I'll just shut down the goddamn foundation. That should resolve any questions about conflicts or fraud," he interrupted.

"…Instead, you used foundation funds for all kinds of personal expenses like paying off that…"

"She was trying to blackmail me," Blount protested. "I was running for President and she was going public with her fake story."

"It doesn't matter," Lawson said. "There were other things. Millions were diverted for your investments and we both know that. And you cannot dismantle the foundation anyway, now that it's the subject of a federal investigation. That would be obstruction of justice. I've told you that at least a dozen times. You've got to listen to people when they give you good advice. Now give me your full attention. The Speaker and the leader of the Senate are here to see you."

"What the hell do they want?"

"Senator Stevens wants to discuss your relationships with certain foreign dictators and Speaker Winstrom is concerned about the public backlash to your immigration policies. They have appointments…"

"Let 'em wait. I want Sissy Nelson in here right now."

"She's on the hill right now. It'll take her a half-hour to get here. Why don't you go ahead and see Stevens and Winstrom? We did give them appointments."

"Yeah, you said that. Let me hear them whine. Send 'em in. and get the Attorney General in here, too."

"That I can do. Mr. Bolin's down the hall right now. You want him before or after Senator Stevens and Speaker Winstrom?"

"During. I want him and "the ghost" in the meeting, too."

"I saw Vice President Gost a few minutes ago, too. I'll get him and Mr. Bolin for you."

Even amid the chaos of the Blount presidency, there still existed a semblance of efficiency for which the White House staff has long been famous. Things didn't run nearly as smoothly as it had in previous administrations. But still, Vice President Wayne "The Ghost" Gost—so-called as much for his creepy omnipresence as for the similarity of his name to that of an apparition—and Attorney General Geoff "The Elf" Bolin were located in short order and marched into the Oval Office along with Stevens and Winstrom, much to the obvious displeasure of the legislators. Forty minutes later, they were joined by Sissy Nelson. Blount was just warming up as she was ushered in.

"Come in, Sissy," he snapped to the Homeland Security Secretary. "I was just outlining my plan to stop the flood of Spicks from pouring into the country."

Nelson glanced at the three men seated in front of Blount. "Sir, I really don't think you should stoop to name-calling. There've been too many leaks to the media from the White House.

"If you think for one nano-second that we're the source of the leaks," Bolin shot back, "then I, in particular, take umbrage at your comment."

"Well, for the record, I don't give a damn if you take umbrage. The leaks are coming from somewhere and until we stop them, we have to be very careful what we say."

"And I really don't care about Spicks if that's what the media gets hold of," Blount said. "I'm sick and tired of these low-lifes sneaking into our country with their drugs, robbing and raping people. That's all they're good for."

Then, looking individually at each of the four, he continued. "Here's what I'm gonna do. "Geoff, I want you and Sissy to get together on this. You find a legal way to do it and Sissy, I expect you to carry out the plan. I promise you, this will stop the illegal entries into the U.S. big

27

time."

Again, Nelson found herself stealing glances at the faces of the other three. Their expressions revealed no emotion or expectations, only mute acceptance and that bothered her.

"I'm signing executive orders that will call for tripling the rent for all federally-assisted housing in the U.S. If they can't pay, evict 'em, shut down the projects. The American taxpayers should not have to support these deadbeats. I'm cutting off Medicaid and food stamp benefits for anyone who lives in these rat holes who doesn't hold a job. Anyone who lives in federally-subsidized housing and isn't working is to surrender their cell phones. If they can't afford to pay for their housing, food and medical care, they have no business owning a cell phone. It's just a tool for drug-dealing and prostitution anyway. And if their kids aren't in school, we'll lock the parents up for neglect and put the kids in juvenile facilities.

"And I want to start separating children from their parents when they enter the country. If that doesn't stop them in their tracks, nothing will. Can you imagine mamas having their babies taken from them if they enter the country illegally? Think about the emotional impact. We won't have to take more than a few hundred before they get the message: We don't want their lazy asses in our country.

"If we shut down the drug-invested federally-subsidized housing by raising their rent and evicting those who won't pay, seize the cell phones and crack down on the illegals entering the country, the drug problems, rapes and murders will go away overnight."

Then, addressing Stevens and Winstrom, he continued. "I want you guys to spearhead legislation to eliminate Meals-on-Wheels and heating fuel assistance. Those old people have families; let them take care of Mommy and Daddy. That's the way it should be, anyway."

Typically, Stevens and Winstrom said nothing. From day one, they had rolled over for Blount in the shameful interest of party unity. It never seemed to matter to them what was the right thing to do—only what was the best face to put forward for the party. Nelson felt a wave of disgust surge through her body. "Sir, I don't think you can do that by fiat. There are civil rights issues at play here. You can't just walk in and seize private property or throw people into the street. And many of these old people on Meals-on-Wheels have no families. The media will eat you

28

alive. And think of the inhumanity of such an action…"

"If they're here illegally, we should be able to do that," Bolin said.

"Waah, waah, waah. I don't give a damn about your 'inhumanity,' or the media," Blount said, glaring at Nelson and coming down heavily on the word "inhumanity" as if mocking her concern for children. "My supporters will love me for it and the media won't like anything I do anyway, so screw them. Your job is to implement the programs the administration puts into place. I'll sign the executive orders and I expect you to carry them out or I'll find someone who will."

"Yes, sir," she answered meekly. Nelson had left an obscure law firm to take the job in Blount's administration with the intention of remaining on the job two or three years before parlaying it into a lucrative job as a network television political analyst. She needed to hang on another year or so in order to solidify her credentials, so it was imperative that she hold onto this job. She had no real choice but to acquiesce to this outrageous demand that she knew would result in serious public outcry.

"Anything else on this matter?" Blount asked, looking at the four faces before him. When no one responded, he dismissed Nelson and then turned to Stevens and Winstrom after instructing Bolin to remain. "Now what was it you gentlemen want to see me about?"

There was an awkward silence as the men watched the door close behind Nelson. "Well, sir," began Stevens, "there's some major concern about your friendship with African dictators who are known to practice genocide." Stevens was called "Pepe Le Peu," or "Stripe," mostly behind his back, because of his solid black hair separated by a single, inch-wide white streak that began at his forehead and ran straight back to his crown. Blount was an exception, deliberately choosing to alternate between the two nicknames as a means of humiliating a perceived subordinate.

"Let me tell you something, Pepe," he said, biting off his words. "I admire strong leaders and these guys are great, strong leaders. I'm loosening the sanctions on their countries because they have assured me they're going to do the right thing—and I believe 'em."

"But, Sir, there's talk that your companies will profit greatly from the natural resources of these countries—diamonds, furs, even ivory which was outlawed until you lifted the restrictions."

"My children run my companies, not me. So, what's the big deal here?

Winstrom shifted nervously from one foot to the other, cleared his throat and said, almost apologetically, "Sir, your children work for you as your advisers. They're part of the administration and as such, running your businesses simultaneously is a blatant conflict of interest."

Blount pounded his desk as he rose to his feet. "Goddamn it, not a single person who voted for me has complained about any conflict. They love everything I do. The only ones who complain are the phony news media hacks. Now unless there's something else on your minds, we're finished here."

Without another word, Stevens and Winstrom, like a pair of admonished schoolchildren, obediently exited the Oval Office. Bolin remained, patiently awaiting the next directive from Blount. It wasn't long coming.

"Get Richter in here," POTUS barked to his submissive attorney general. Liz Lawson, who had lingered quietly in the background the entire time, didn't wait for Bolin to act. She whipped out her cell phone and hit Callahan's number on her speed dial and instructed him to report to the Oval Office ASAP. Bolin appeared chagrined at having been upstaged by the Chief of Staff but said nothing. She reminded him of a scavenger, patiently waiting for the appearance of a carrion on which to feed. From that perspective, he thought she was perfect for her job.

Wolfe Richter was cut from the same cloth, Bolin thought, but dared not say aloud. Of German heritage, Richter served as Blount's political advisor for policy and most observers felt that a worse choice would have been impossible. But Blount loved his far-right leanings and called on him often for policy directions, especially in dealing with racial matters. Invariably, those decisions exploded as public relations disasters in the opinions of all but Blount's tight-knit cadre of his most fervent supporters, the rabid, hate-spewing white supremist splinter groups.

When Richter was heckled by protestors at a Washington D.C. restaurant, called among the more civil terms employed, racist and fascist, Blount supporters peppered the restaurant's Web page with poor ratings even though the critics had never set foot inside the restaurant's doors. It seemed particularly ironic that Richter, the despised architect of Blount's blatantly anti-Hispanic immigration policies, would choose to dine in a Mexican restaurant. But then, irony appeared to have been lost on this administration long ago.

Richter metaphorically would take Blount's hand and guide it, pen in hand, across the paper as new executive orders, directing ever-increasing restrictions on basic rights, were drafted. Again, as with nearly all of Blount's actions, irony was at play with each new executive order. One of the biggest complaints against his predecessor, Hiram Weinberg, a Jew, was that he issued too many executive orders. Blount easily surpassed Weinberg's eight-year total number of executive orders in his first year in office. Almost without exception, each was aimed at eradicating some action implemented by Weinberg whose biggest sin in Blount's viewpoint appeared to be that he was Weinberg. Much to the delight of his maniacal base, he refused to even try to conceal his contempt for his predecessor, in fact seeming to revel in it.

Many of the other choices for top positions in his administration were of no better caliber. They ranged from the inept to the clueless to the outright corrupt. Some of the appointees who warranted closer vetting by the Senate but were nevertheless confirmed included:

- Former U.S. Rep. Octavius Munson, Interior Secretary. He would prove his loyalty to Blount with his advocacy for the development of public lands, exploration of offshore oil and gas production, and the shrinkage of federally-protected land. Munson also favored the seizure of yet more land from Native Americans already living on reservations to which they'd been consigned when their land was taken from them in the nineteenth century. Munson wanted what land they had left for oil and gas exploration but any consideration of sharing royalties with the tribes was taken off the table. It was, after all, federal land. The white man's federal land.
- Wesley Foulks, Commerce Secretary. A billionaire, he had amassed the bulk of his fortune heading up a European bank that specialized in laundering money for Russian oligarchs.
- Robert Thomas, Treasury Secretary. Another billionaire who came from Wall Street, his duties included revamping the federal tax code that would favor the very wealthy while placing the bulk of the tax burden on the American middle class while telling them they would be the beneficiaries. It was an easy sell. Despite charges that he operated a bank that was overly aggres-

sive in foreclosing on homes, he was confirmed by a compliant Senate.

- Wesley Wright, a former U.S. Representative, Director of the Office of Management and Budget. He would work diligently to remove eligible recipients from Medicaid. Following his confirmation, he would confide to a group of bankers that while serving as a member of the House, the only lobbyists he met with were those who made "substantial" political contributions to his campaign.

- Larry Rogers, Environmental Protection Agency Administrator. Easily the most controversial of Blount's appointments, Rogers appeared to be competing with his boss for negative headlines on an almost daily basis. From exorbitant expenditures for his office to living in a home provided by a lobbyist, to assigning subordinates to run menial personal errands, and accepting European vacation trips, Rogers just didn't seem to be able to distinguish the difference between a job where he was supposed to work on behalf of the American people to holding a position for personal gain. Demands for his resignation actually outnumbered those for Blount's impeachment.

- Sandra Healy, Education Secretary. Healy possessed no qualifications whatever for the job. Yet, she was confirmed by the Senate after contentious hearings. Her only job in the real world involved operating a company that bordered on a pyramid scheme. Her plans for the Department of Education were focused on the privatization of public education to the exclusion of everything else.

- Scott Rankin, Secretary of Housing and Urban Development. A one-time candidate for the nomination eventually captured by Blount, Rankin vowed during his confirmation hearings that he would never advocate the abolition of safety net programs without offering an alternative. Yet, once ensconced in office, he did precisely that—at Blount's direction, of course.

6

The day broke beautifully over the Atlantic. Clouds were nowhere to be seen, the temperature was in the mid-sixties. Gulls and pelicans floated easily against the gentle breeze. Occasionally one of the pelicans would go into a sudden dive when he spotted food swimming near the surface of the calm ocean waters. Despite the overall lack of interest as a nation, there are the ever-faithful who attempt to watch every launch. So, the usual gathering of launch groupies had parked along the highways and on the beach. They had come to watch the eight hundred-ton rocket, propelled by eight million pounds, or four thousand tons, of combined thrust from its three RS-25 engines, climb into the azure sky before disappearing from sight in less than two minutes—not much longer than it takes to watch a horse race, but considerably more intense.

The seven crew members, each of us holding our helmet under our arm and smiling and waving to news photographers and NASA support personnel with the other, emerged from the final briefing room onto the long ramp that would take us to the Sol Orbiter One. Cheers of the well-wishers went up as we exited into the cool morning sunlight. No words were spoken by any of us. There was a tenseness behind our smiles that no one could possibly appreciate. This was not a *Star Trek* episode but admittedly, the trite thought, uttered at the beginning of each episode of the show, did pop into my head: we were truly going where no man had gone before. Each of us was secured in an impenetrable mental cocoon of deeply private thoughts of the unknown perils that lay ahead. We were also absorbed with the sobering realization that the success of the mission and the lives of the entire crew depended upon each member carrying out assignments flawlessly.

Ground crews in Houston and Cape Canaveral had been briefed so many times they could recite their functions in their sleep. So could we. No detail, no conceivable scenario was overlooked or glossed over or taken as routine. There would be the harrowing time, within minutes of achieving orbit, not around the earth but around the sun, that radio contact would be lost for most of the four-month duration of the mission. That was the most frightening prospect of all—not knowing what was going on with the crew for such an extended period of time. Everyone had been prepared for that condition as much as possible but it still was an unsteadying proposition for technicians accustomed to unbroken radio contact with crews in previous missions. For the bulk of the entire mission, ground control would be absolutely powerless to advise or otherwise assist the Sol Orbiter One crew.

****

The tradition established in previous missions was for the President to make an obligatory telephone call of encouragement to the crew in the hours before launch. In this case, consistent with his radical non-traditional approach, President Andrus Blount offered not even a tweet of good luck wishes to the seven. Never before had a Chief Executive chosen to simply ignore a manned mission. It was considered by the media already growing increasingly critical of Blount as a serious breach of protocol and they lost no time playing it up on their Internet web pages. But to tell the God's truth, we could not have cared less. He was, after all, the provocateur-in-chief.

But Blount was too preoccupied with the next way to promote himself to spare the time to acknowledge seven Americans who were about to risk our lives on a mission into the true unknown void of space. His tweets did go out as usual, but instead of wishing us Godspeed, they consisted of his criticisms of anyone who disagreed with him, including members of his own political party, and messages to his ever-shrinking base about what a great leader he was. Such a narcissist was he that he could never see—or at least, could never admit—that nearly a year into his administration, every piece of legislation he had backed had failed miserably and that he had yet to fulfill a single campaign promise. Still, he boasted of non-existent accomplishments.

andrusblount@Verified account@POTUS.com: *more accomplished in first year than any other president in history.*

Given, a year is a short time frame in which to hold an elected official to campaign promises, but Blount had made such a point during his campaign of repeating that many of the things he planned to do, he would do "during my first day in office" through Executive Orders. But even those had failed to materialize. Nor had he delivered on his promise to produce his income tax returns. Many critics speculated that was because of his illegal business dealings with foreign governments before and during his campaign for the presidency and right up to his taking the oath of office—and beyond. Strangely though, no one in Congress stepped forward to call his hand with any definitive authority. No one in his inner circle seemed able—or willing—to rein him in on his increasingly irrational behavior and this only emboldened him to keep pushing the envelope on domestic issues and foreign relations. His unpredictable mood swings, erratic tweets and public utterances kept both friend and foe off balance. As he careened from one idiotic, devastatingly thoughtless remark to the next potentially disastrous directive, the farthest things from his mind was the fate of seven people whose names he did not even know who were preparing to blast into space.

andrusblount@Verified account@POTUS.com: *second thoughts about sec state, att gen. weak willed men.*

I had never expected anything in the way of leadership from Blount, who was far too self-absorbed to ever think of anyone but himself. But the members of Congress, with their collective cowardice, their fear of confronting Blount, and for the majority's transparent, partisan priority to party unity over the overall good of the country, were an even greater disappointment than usual. It occurred to me that there was not a single one of the entire bunch who I would ever give any consideration to accepting as a crew member for even the simplest of missions, let alone one this dangerous. I could just never place my fate in their unsteady, unreliable hands.

****

Before I get into the details of the mission itself, there's something you should know about launches and g-forces. First of all, the term g-force is technically incorrect since it is actually a measure of acceleration, not force. As one might deduce, the letter *g* comes from gravitation. The term refers to a type of acceleration. Gravitation alone doesn't produce a g-force, even though the term is expressed in multiples of the acceleration of a standard gravity. G-force accelerations indirectly produce weight.

If a g-force is vertically upward as, say, in an elevator, and is applied to the ground, most of the body experiences compressive stress which is related to the mechanical force. If you are on an elevator, especially one of those express elevators in high-rise buildings, you feel the effects of g-force when the elevator car begins its ascent. You begin to feel the effects of accelerated g-force, for example, in a dragster where you can experience a horizontal g-force of 5.3. But you can feel g-forces in the opposite direction as well. The g-force acting on the human body under acceleration may be downward such as when cresting a sharp hill on a roller coaster.

Of course, the effect is not nearly as extreme at elevator or dragster speeds as when you're involved in a collision. That's when the g-force can be critical even during a short duration. But if you're strapped in a rocket being propelled into space, it can get pretty dicey then because you not only experience extreme g-forces, but you do so for an extended period of time.

The human body's tolerance depends on the magnitude of the g-force, the length of time it is applied, the direction it acts, the location of the application, and the posture of the body. All these factors must be taken into account by NASA, and crew members must go through rigorous training to determine their fitness to withstand the phenomenon.

The human body, particularly the soft tissue area, is flexible. A sharp slap to the face, for example, creates hundreds of g in a small area of the body but does not result in any real damage. But a prolonged force of sixteen g, say for a minute, can be lethal. When experienced with vibration, even relatively low peak g levels can be quite damaging should they occur at the resonance frequency of organs or connective tissues.

Pilots (and astronauts) experience g-forces along the axis aligned with the spine, causing significant variation in blood pressure along the entire length of the pilot's body. This places limitations on the maximum g-forces which can be tolerated by an individual. Positive, or upward g-forces drive blood downward to the feet of a seated or standing person. Typically, a person can endure a force of about five-g but when wearing special g-suits we can usually handle a sustained nine-g force. Vertical g-forces, such as that experienced by astronauts, are usually positive in that blood is forced toward the feet and away from the head. This can cause temporary loss of vision, tunnel vision, or loss of consciousness. Even death can occur if g-forces are not quickly reduced.

This is why we are strapped into our seats in a horizonal position. It enables us to better survive g-forces that are perpendicular to the spine. This position is known to astronauts as "eyeballs in," and gives us a much higher tolerance.

At a liftoff speed of about five miles per second, a six-g force for half-a-minute has been documented by NASA. And all that is just for the launch. Re-entry accelerations are even greater and can produce a force of nearly eight-g on the body.

So, you can understand why Blount's shenanigans were the furthest thing from our minds as we walked up that ramp and into the shuttle.

7

"Colonel Whitten, there's something you need to see."

It was Lieutenant Colonel Damon, Wilhite, the pilot speaking as he roused me from a light sleep.

The launch had gone off without a hitch and we were now two months into our projected four-month orbit of the sun. We had been spending the time floating around the cabin in the zero-gravity atmosphere performing our tasks which by now had become routine. I, along with the rest of the crew, was lying in my bunk resting when Damon roused me from my sleep.

I looked up at the pilot quizzically and unbuckled the straps that held me in place in my bunk where the crew members slept in their respective quarters. "Whatcha got?" I asked as I floated along behind Wilhite through the cramped cabin.

"I don't want to wake the others just yet," Wilhite whispered. "I want you to see this first." We continued through the maze of the ship's computers, gauges, and life-support systems. Looking out into the vastness of space, there was little to distinguish the vista from the millions of miles we had already traveled. The entire crew, initially overcome by the magnificence and beauty of infinite space, had long since become accustomed to the monotony of it all as we settled into the routine of our individual tasks. The unchanging view, while breathtaking at first, had become repetitive after two months. After only a few days, there was no longer the awe-struck fascination and we had settled into the routine professionalism that had earned us our selection for the mission in the first place.

That isn't to say that the vastness of infinite space couldn't still overwhelm us and remind us of our relative insignificance in the greater scheme that is the universe. Viewing the Earth and the stars from one's imagined perspective of God, be it the Christian, Judaism, or Hindu version—each of which was represented in our crew—is something you never get used to or take for granted. There was no way anyone could have prepared us for the grandeur, the vastness, and the overpowering beauty of space. To simply say the splendor induced a reverence you never knew was possible is to woefully understate the obvious.

It's called the "overview effect," and it was first articulated in 1987 by author Frank White, who said it was the sudden realization that we live on a planet. Shuttle astronauts had their own descriptions. Jeff Hoffman said one not only sees the Earth as a planet, but the sun as a star. "…Up there, you see the sun in a black sky…from the cosmic perspective." Nicole Stott said, "I don't know how you can come back and not, in some way, be changed. I think, collectively, everybody has that emblazoned on their memories, the way the planet looks."

"When we look down at the Earth from space," said Ron Garan, "we see this amazing, indescribably beautiful planet. It looks like a living, breathing organism. But it also, at the same time, looks extremely fragile."

Alan Shepard, the first American to travel in space and at age forty-seven, the oldest person to walk on the moon, said, "If somebody'd said before the flight, 'Are you going to get carried away looking at the Earth from the moon?' I would have said, 'No, no way.' But yet, when I first looked back at the earth, standing on the moon, I cried."

Taylor Wang, the first ethnic Chinese person to travel into space, said, "A Chinese tale tells of some men sent to harm a young girl who, upon seeing her beauty, became her protectors rather than her violators. That how I felt seeing the Earth for the first time. I could not help but love and cherish her."

Even poets, politicians and philosophers who have never traveled in space, could appreciate the image. Archibald MacLeish, in his Christmas Day, 1968, *New York Times* essay, wrote, "To see the earth as it truly is, small and blue and beautiful in that eternal silence where it floats, is to see ourselves as riders on the earth together, brothers on that bright loveliness in the eternal cold—brothers who know now they are truly brothers."

Long before even the Wright brothers took that experimental leap at Kitty Hawk, men fantasized about space. Galileo, in 1632, said prophetically, "If you could see the earth illuminated when you were in a place as dark as night, it would look to you more splendid than the moon."

Plato, in 342 B.C., said, "Astronomy compels the soul to look upward, and leads us from this world to another." In 30 B.C., Cicero said, "The contemplation of celestial things will make a man both speak and think more sublimely and magnificently when he descends to human affairs."

In 1958, the year after the Soviet launching of Sputnik, scientist Wernher von Braun, the "Father of Space Flight," wrote, "There is beauty in space, and it is orderly. There is no weather, and there is regularity. Everything in space obeys the laws of physics."

Sally Ride, the first American woman in space, blasted into history on June 18, 1983, as radio stations across the nation played Wilson Pickett's *Mustang Sally* but Ride herself did not appreciate the magnitude of her accomplishment until later. "On launch day, there was so much excitement and so much happening around us in crew quarters, even on the way to the launch pad," she said in a 2008 interview commemorating the 25th anniversary of her flight. "I didn't really think about it that much at the time but I came to appreciate what an honor it was to be selected to be the first to get a chance to go into space."

Marsha Ivins, said of her five space shuttle missions, said space travel isn't glamorous, "but you can't beat the view." It isn't just a series of breathtaking moments, she said, "it's a mix of transcendently magical and the deeply prosaic."

It's strange how we manage to pick the occasions to reflect on such things but these were the thoughts that swirled through my brain as I followed Wilhite. We are supposed to be disciplined professionals, trained to focus on a single task. But we are also human and now my mind was clicking off the possible scenarios that could prompt Wilhite to rouse me from needed sleep.

Astronauts, contrary to popular misconception, aren't necessarily nervous while sitting atop several million pounds of explosive rocket fuel on the launchpad. For two hours after climbing into the shuttle, many astronauts actually take naps while they're strapped in as the system goes through thousands of pre-launch checks.

Zero-gravity can cause astronauts to get severe headaches and to experience nausea. The body loses about a liter of fluid in the first couple days in space as the crew finds that the best headache remedy is urinating. All space food is pre-cooked and either freeze-dried and vacuum-packed or thermos-stabilized, like a military MRE.

Sleep in space took some getting used to. Sleeping bags were strapped to the wall, ceiling or floor—it didn't matter in zero-gravity—and we climbed in. We extended our arms through armholes so we could zip up the bag from the outside. Then we tightened Velcro straps around our bodies to create the feeling of being tucked in. Did you ever have to strap your head to your pillow? We did. Finally, we found it necessary to tuck our arms into the bag lest they drift out in front of our bodies. It's quite a weird feeling to wake up and see your arm floating in front of your face.

And, of course, there is the problem of going to the bathroom. Flushing a household toilet in space would be nothing short of disastrous—and disgusting. Space toilets are equipped with a thigh bar similar to those on roller coasters. And they serve the same purpose—holding the occupant in place. The toilet, instead of using water for flushing, uses air which pulls waste away from the astronaut's body. The air is filtered to remove bacteria and odors and returned to the living cabin while solid wastes are dried to remove moisture, compressed and held in an on-board storage container to be removed and disposed of once the spacecraft has landed. Liquid wastes are recycled through a special water treatment plant and turned back into drinking water.

All those thoughts, in one form or another, weaved their way through our brains as we shared the same experiences and discomforts as previous astronauts. But we had jobs to do and we couldn't spend every waking minute as gawking tourists, so we worked most of the time and admired the breathtaking splendor of it all when we could.

It's only when everything settles into a routine that our minds tend to wander.

So, it was against this disciplined normalcy that my natural curiosity was piqued. What was the reason for the pilot's sudden urgency? Many thoughts raced through my mind as we glided effortlessly toward the front of the shuttle. Was something malfunctioning? Was there an oxygen leak? Why would he not wake Nguyen Huy or Sarah Bergmann if the computers crashed? Or Rafael Vasquez or Daryl Booth if there was a mechanical or electrical failure? If someone had fallen ill, that would necessitate alerting Dr. Hubballi Patel immediately. I couldn't comprehend the urgency of my being alerted while the others were allowed to rest.

As the two of us settled into our seats at the controls of the gigantic shuttle, Wilhite pointed straight ahead. "Look," he said. "See that?"

At first, I saw nothing out of the ordinary, ordinary being a relative term in the endless void that is space. But then I caught the image of a tiny blue ball, slightly larger than the surrounding stars, emerging from the vastness. I bolted upright, my full attention focused on the planet, still a quarter of a million miles away. "Is that Earth?" I asked. "It can't be."

"Sure looks like it to me," Wilhite replied.

"It can't be," I repeated. "We're still two months out from our rendezvous."

"That's why I woke you up. The calculations don't have us hooking up for seventy-three more days. This is crazy."

Simultaneously, we became aware that the other crew members were gathering behind us, curious about what was going on. Somehow, almost as one, they had sensed something was amiss even though not a word had passed between them and their pilot and myself. It was Rafael Vasquez, the mechanical engineer, who spoke first. "What's up, Colonel? We got a problem?

For the moment I ignored Vasquez, choosing first to address Bergmann. "Sarah, double check our location and rendezvous time for me, will you?" No one else spoke while Bergmann ran the figures. It took her only a few minutes and she returned to the rest. "Colonel, we're seventeen hundred, sixty-one hours from rendezvous. That's seventy-three days, nine hours. We're approximately seventy days from being able to establish radio contact with Houston."

"Check again," I said.

Perplexed, Bergmann obliged, retiring back to her computers. Her second answer was the same as the first. "I come up with the same figures that Houston calculated," she said. "seventeen hundred, sixty-one hours. Is something wrong?"

I leaned back in my seat and pointed to the small blue circle. "What does your computer say that is?" I asked—not in a sarcastic manner but with a combination of honest curiosity and confusion.

Bergmann's mouth flew open. "Tha...that can't be! It's impossible! We're still more than two months out!"

The four others pushed forward to see. Each crew member had the same incredulous reaction. They alternated between staring at each other and the blue ball ahead of them, nearly inaudible gasps escaping their lips. "What the hell does this mean?" It was electrical engineer Daryl Booth. "None of our systems have malfunctioned," he said. "Everything has gone picture-perfect on the mission. Not a hiccup. How can we be hooking up this quickly?"

"Beats me," I said. "I'm as baffled by this as you are." Then, turning my back to the crew, I attempted radio contact for the first time in nearly two months.

"Houston, this is Sol Orbiter One. We've got you in our sights. Over."

No response.

"Houston, do you read?"

Nothing.

"Houston, this is Sol Orbiter One. Can you confirm we're a couple of months early for our date?"

Silence from both the ship's radio and from her crew. No one spoke for a full minute. Finally, it was Bergmann who broke the eerie stillness of the shuttle. "We appear to still be a couple of days away. Let me try a few things with the computer."

"Go ahead," I said. "I'll keep trying to get somebody on the radio. If we're as early as everyone thinks, hell, they could all be asleep down there." My feeble attempt at humor fell flat as no one among the crew so much as smiled. They all—we all—knew something was definitely not right. Engineers, mathematicians and computers just don't make mistakes of such proportions.

For the next two days—forty-eight straight hours, given there are no "days" in space— Wilhite and I alternated at our attempts to establish radio contact as the blue ball grew from a tiny circle to a full-blown planet with the oceans and continents coming more and more into focus. Sleep was all but impossible. The entire crew cat-napped at best as each went about his or her duties with the mystery of the early rendezvous and absence of radio contact looming over our heads like an ominous, dark cloud.

As the crew prepared for our final approach, I had an idea that, while posing considerable risks, might offer some explanation of something, anything. "Colonel Wilhite, could you take her around a couple of times so we can get a look? I've got a weird feeling about this."

"You and me both, Colonel," Wilhite answered. "Stand by for the nickel tour."

As Wilhite navigated, the Sol Orbiter One orbited the planet twice as the crew surveyed a world in ruins. What once were obviously magnificent buildings were reduced to rubble. Entire cities lay in total ruin. Vast areas that appeared to have once been fertile farmlands now stood barren, brown and eroded. There were few trees, mostly burned remnants, really, twisted, scarred, and broken. There were no aircraft aloft though the remains of large commercial airports, pitted with gaping holes, were in evidence. Nor were there any ships on the seas even though what appeared to have been thriving shipping terminals now lay twisted and abandoned along the coastlines of what had been major seaport cities. Crippled ocean liners lay half submerged, most toppled onto their sides like giant, dead beasts. Nothing moved below.

"*Dios Mio,*" whispered Vasquez under his breath as he surveyed the unbelievable destruction below him.

As we made a pass over what appeared to be the remains of Houston, I said to Wilhite, "Hold us in place until we can launch the LEM and then take her back up and out of the Earth's gravitational pull."

"Aye, aye, Colonel." His tone was flat, devoid of emotion. He was doing his best to maintain a calm demeanor but I knew he was as baffled and afraid as the rest of us.

"Roger that," he said as if he had failed to answer the first time, realizing that I was trying to conserve the shuttle's limited fuel which, while not really an issue outside the Earth's gravitational pull, would be spent more quickly while orbiting the unknown planet. Once free of Earth's gravity, solar cells were all that were needed to thrust the crew deeper into space.

I called out to Vasquez and Booth. "Get the LEM ready for launch," I said.

The LEM, an acronym for Lunar Excursion Module, would carry a skeleton crew to the Earth's surface so that we could hopefully get some answers.

Turning back to Wilhite, I said, "I'll have my radio so at least we can communicate. Take her up until you hear from me."

"What if I don't hear from you? What then?"

I smiled as best I could through my obvious concern. "Well, I guess that'll be your call. That's our home down there, or at least what's left of it. I don't know what has happened in the two months we've been gone, but we can both see it ain't pretty. If you don't hear from me, your only alternative will be to land this bird and try to survive on your own."

"Colonel...." Wilhite's voice trailed off.

"What?" I was already concentrating on getting the LEM prepared for launch and didn't look Wilhite's way.

"Colonel, what the hell's this?"

I turned to see Wilhite peering out the front of the shuttle. "Sir, are there two moons up here?"

We had observed a moon orbiting the planet as we approached and thought nothing of it. After all, moon walks by astronauts were old hat by now. But now Wilhite was pointing to a second, smaller satellite. I follow his gaze and muttered, "What the hell? Bergmann! Get up here!"

Bergmann had been hard at work at her computers and was coming up with conclusions of her own when she heard the flight commander call. "Sir, I have a theory you're not going to belie...."

"I know what you're gonna say," I interrupted. "Look at this! I don't know where we are, but we aren't on Earth. We don't have two moons."

Bergmann barely looked up from her calculation printouts as she continued. "I know, sir. I know this sounds screwy, but I think we've stumbled upon a sister planet we never knew about, one that's in our same orbital path, traveling the same speed as Earth, but one hundred eighty degrees from Earth. We never saw it because it's always on the other side of the sun."

"Impossible," said Dr. Hubballi Patel, the shuttle physician.

"Bullshit!" said Booth.

"I think she's right," volunteered Nguyen Huy. She had been running her own computer programs since the tiny blue ball was first spotted by the crew. "We're less than two months into a four-month mission. There's no way we could be rendezvousing with Earth this soon. This is a major discovery, if true."

"Get that damned LEM ready!" I barked. "Vasquez, Nguyen,

come with me."

"Hey! What am I, chopped liver?" Booth said, practically yelling. "I want to see what's down there."

"Booth, we have to have someone on board the shuttle who can handle the electrical systems. You're needed here. Same with you, Bergmann. Sorry." Turning to Wilhite, I said, "If we lose radio contact for any reason or we're not back in forty-eight hours, assume the worst and resume the mission."

"Roger," Wilhite replied.

Nguyen, Vasquez, and I said our goodbyes as we prepared to board the LEM for its descent onto the surface of what we all now assumed was Earth's sister planet. For what we knew about what lay in wait for us, we may as well have been entering some sort of parallel universe, which, in a way, we were.

8

The administration of Andrus Blount was off to a rocky start, much of his initial troubles attributable to his own combative persona, his insatiable need for approval, and his urge to take to twitter over any slight, any insult, that he felt impugned his own twisted sense of honor. To be sure, it was a sense of honor shared by a precious few outside his hardcore supporters which only a few months into his term had shrunk to thirty-four percent of voters.

His narcissistic personality disorder, which bordered on psychopathy, demanded unconditional approval of his inner circle and that approval bled over to that thirty-four percent concentrated mainly in the deep South and Midwest, creating a recipe for disaster that was soon in coming.

The only sense of entitlement Blount recognized was that of white males to make the rules by which all others must play. Blacks, Hispanics, Islamic, and women were grouped together into a sub-class that had no voice in its own destiny. As Blount issued calls for cuts to programs that benefitted minorities and the poor, his base rallied to the call, oblivious to the fact that those very cuts were averse to their own interests. But then, mass hypnosis rarely involves rational thought.

Blount made no attempt to conceal his contempt for those whom he considered inferior to himself. Narcissism, after all, is a mental condition in which individuals are marked by an inflated sense of their own importance. That sense is coupled with a unquenchable need for excessive attention and admiration and a lack of empathy for others. Thus, his ego was fed by the extreme actions of his rabid political base and the subservient support of his inner circle that which was in a constant state of flux, depending upon whom he distrusted on a given day.

It reached a crescendo on a balmy day in Alabama when a white supremist leader named Carlos Whalen held a rally at a public park in Birmingham. When civil rights groups turned out to protest the rally, events quickly spun out of control as rednecks carrying clubs, knives, and guns waded into their counterparts and blood was spilled onto the green grass and into the street. By the time police managed to break up the melee, four people from the civil rights group were dead and hundreds of others from both sides suffered injuries that varied from bruises and abrasions to cuts and gunshot wounds.

Despite the fact that only one group was armed, Blount immediately took to twitter to condemn the civil rights demonstrators as comprised of "thugs and a criminal element" while characterizing Whalen's followers as patriots and "good, decent Americans" whose right to assemble and voice their opinion was undermined by "violent criminals."

But network television cameras had captured the entire scene and video evidence clearly showed who the aggressors were. The more the newscasts showed the perpetrators to be Whalen's bullies, the more Blount dug his heels in. His twitter messages became increasingly accusatory as he lashed out at news reporters as "enemies of America" and at the peaceful protestors as being something less than human.

The attack on the media only served to galvanize reporters' resolve to resist the man they considered to be a tyrant and he in turn, ramped up the rhetoric, hurling personal insults at individual reporters. The exchange further fueled violence. Black churches and mosques were bombed or burned to the ground. Shots were fired into newspaper offices and random attacks on people with dark skin increased exponentially.

Even as the fires of racial hatred were being fanned by Blount, controversy was emerging on another front as women, emboldened by their contempt for the president, came forward with harrowing tales of sexual harassment by Blount, members of Congress and executives throughout the business world. The charges were not with their intended effects. Heads rolled as one after another of the accused either resigned in disgrace or was forced into weak denials of the accusations. Blount was not spared by the accusers. A dozen women related their experience with the man they described as an ogre and some even offered audio recordings of his boasts of sexual dominance over women.

Blount, true to his nature, went on the attack, even proposing at one point that the solution to sexual harassment charges in the business world was to simply not hire women in the future. His tweets were particularly insensitive and insulting:

andrusblount@Verified account@POTUS.com: *men are more reliable, more loyal, and much, much more intelligent.*

andrusblount@Verified account@POTUS.com: *They don't get pregnant, they don't have PMS, they don't cry. Boo-hoo.*

This, of course, infuriated women everywhere and women's rights organizations and women in Congress went ballistic even as Blount's redneck base cheered and clinked their beer bottles together in barroom toasts and evangelicals received his utterances as gospel, sent down to Earth from heaven above. It was a curious marriage of ideals indeed.

All of this only intensified the war of words between Blount and his perceived enemies, the media being the principal adversary. As the media allowed itself to be pulled into the exchanges of charges and counter-charges swirling around these matters, Blount was achieving his goal of deflecting attention from the main issue: charges he had colluded with foreign powers to win the election to the most powerful position on the planet. With increasing regularity, daily press briefings by his office devolved into verbal skirmishes with White House press secretary Darla Rutledge.

The veteran reporters who tried to cut through the smokescreen and to focus on the larger picture feared that Blount was descending into madness. His rants against long-standing allies, criticisms of his own intelligence agencies, his tweet storms and his clumsy attempts to curry favor from longtime adversaries only served to stoke that fear. His non-stop sword-rattling against Mideast nations that he threatened to "annihilate back to the Stone Age" left career diplomats in the State Department shaking their heads in disbelief.

At the same time that he was systematically dismantling social programs and environmental protection regulations and eliminating safeguards that had been imposed on freewheeling Wall Street investment bankers and hedge funds, there was at the same time a far more sinister—and furtive—development taking place. Local law enforcement agencies were quietly being equipped with armaments originally intended to fight wars on an international scale.

He initiated a policy of updating military hardware—tanks, armored personnel vehicles, rocket launchers, automatic weapons, assault vehicles and armored helicopters. As the old equipment was replaced and updated, the old armaments, officially termed "obsolete" but still effectively lethal, were doled out to even the smallest municipal and college police departments throughout the country. Even places where no perceivable threat existed began flexing their newfound muscle. Police chiefs and sheriffs posed proudly in local newspapers with their added kill power. There was only one purpose for equipping the local agencies: to put down civil disturbances that Blount knew would one day take place. Even in his state of advanced mental impairment, he was keenly aware that he could go only so far in taking benefits and rights from the people before they would rise up in revolt.

And he would be ready when the moment came.

He was fully prepared—and willing—to suspend the election now less than three years away. Unwilling to risk losing his bid for a second term, he was already formulating a plan for marshal law, backed up with all that military hardware now in the hands of loyal police chiefs nationwide, and to declare himself as the permanent president, the first dictator in the nation's history.

To hedge his bets, he set about forming his own secret police force, reminiscent of Hitler's Schutzstaffel (SS), and independent of the FBI and CIA but with the autonomy to carry out the mission of both domestic and foreign espionage. No independent news organization would be safe. No electronic communications would be exempt from prying eyes—not email, texts, or any other form of correspondence. Blount would be able to readily access any citizen's private tax or medical records. Americans would, under his plan, hear only the news he desired them to hear, filtered through his own news agency.

Professionals intimately familiar with narcissistic personality disorder were not distracted from those stealthy developments. Rather than focus on Blount's tweets and political rhetoric, they were consumed by the fear that his constant battles with the media, liberals, minorities, more moderate members of his own political party, all of which were chipping away at his approval ratings, would compel him into starting a "wag-the-dog" war in order to bring his poll numbers up. It was a chilling prospect in light of the fear that he would not be content with conventional warfare, bad enough in its own right, but that he might well launch a nuclear attack against some designated threat, throwing the world into nuclear holocaust.

Most troubling of all, his plan was advancing at what for Washington was considered warp speed. No one rose up to stand in his way, to say you can't do that, it's unconstitutional. Opponents, the few who existed, withered under the barrage of verbal attacks from his boisterous supports among the citizenry and in Congress.

The Sol Orbiter One crew had only an inkling of what was developing as they hurdled through space at one hundred forty thousand miles per hour on their orbit around the sun. Of the seven crew members, four had voted for Blount's opponent but they rarely discussed politics among themselves. Whitten harbored a secret ambition to seek political office once he retired from his military career, probably the U.S. Senate, though he had shared that desire with no one, not even immediate family members. All that would come later. There would be ample time to survey the political landscape once the mission was complete. For now, though, there was other, more pressing work to be done.

But back home, the Blount administration was careening from crisis to crisis as the media struggled to keep up with developments.

9

Wilhite selected a small area south of what we had thought
at first to be Houston. The area, closer to where Galveston would have
been back home, appeared relatively flat—and desolate. Unlike Houston,
though, the terrain immediately in the direction we presumed to be the
west was hilly, similar to the hill country outside Austin. Our chosen
landing area abutted a vast body of water similar to Earth's Gulf of Mexico. The fact there was water on the planet gave support to the possibility of life. The crew had observed from Sol Orbiter One's passes that
some sort of advanced civilization had once inhabited the land below.
Skeletons of skyscrapers and other buildings reached skyward like silent
ghouls. What at an earlier time were obviously highways and rail lines
now lay twisted and cratered. Some of the buildings, along with stretch-
es of railways, and highways disappeared into waters that covered what
appeared to have once been land masses. What plant life there was struggling to survive in a hostile atmosphere despite its proximity to water.

As the LEM settled onto the parched ground amid equally
scorched mountains that surrounded us, Nguyen, Vasquez, and I could
feel our pulses accelerating in anticipation of the unknown discoveries
that awaited us. In an abundance of caution, we each wore our customized extravehicular suits, pressurized to provide us with oxygen. Each
suit also contained a massive network of wiring and bearings that allowed us to remain in radio contact with Sol Orbiter One—and Houston,
had we been in radio range of Earth—and provided surprising flexibility
to perform necessary functions. Our gloves were individually cast for

perfect fits to facilitate the use of our fingers.

Despite efforts to provide custom fits for each individual, walking remained a task that proved cumbersome. As we explored in different directions, little was said. There was nothing extraordinary about the surrounding landscape other than the fact that there was little, if any, living vegetation. Suddenly, Nguyen broke the silence.

"Nine o'clock, sir."

As best I could in my bulky pressurized suit, I executed a clumsy quarter-turn to my left and saw a thin plume of dust drifting into the air just beyond a grove of what may once have been healthy scrub trees before they had given up and surrendered to whatever it was that robbed the area of virtually all vegetation. Most of what remained were charred tree trunks and a few broken, dead limbs.

As the three of us watched, the dust cloud grew nearer until finally a lone figure on horseback emerged from the gnarled stand of trees. Though the horse was approaching at a trot, its pace was deliberate but cautious, as if prepared to change direction at full speed if need be. Under my breath, I muttered to the others, "Hold your place and don't make any sudden moves." Vasquez, despite his apprehension over the approaching rider, couldn't stifle a smile. *How can we make any sudden moves in this get-up?*

Thirty feet away, the rider pulled his mount to a halt. The poor animal looked half-starved, its ribs trying to protrude through its matted hide. The rider didn't look much better. An ugly, hand-crafted patch covered his left eye and a scraggly beard tumbled down upon his bare, concave chest. When he opened his mouth, the astronauts observed only a couple of teeth. His first words scared the hell out of us: "Приветствия. Вы по-русски?" *Greetings. Are you Russian?*

Each of us was fluent in Russian; it's one of the requirements to becoming an astronaut. Nevertheless, we were astounded. I somehow managed to respond: "Нет, мы." *No, we're American.* My brain raced to process the exchange. How did he know what a Russian was, let alone speak the language? At first, I tried to consider the odds of the rider comprehending what an American was, but then, if he knew what a Russian was….

"Well, in any case, welcome to *Terranum,* or as you would say of your world, Earth" the rider said in perfect English. "We've been expecting you for some time. I assume our conversation is being monitored up there," he said, looking toward the heavens. "That's fine. We have much to tell you and the more ears that hear our story, the better." He dismounted and approached to shake hands with each of us. "Please come with me," he said as he began leading his horse back toward the direction from which he had approached us. "You'll be welcome in our village."

We exchanged nervous glances as we fell in behind him, unsure of what lay ahead.

****

Aboard Sol Orbiter One, Wilhite, Patel, Bergmann, and Booth were transfixed. *What the hell's going on down there?* Wilhite was thinking. *What did they stumble upon?*

Patel was hoping her crewmates would re-board the LEM and return immediately before something terrible happened. Her thoughts were only of their safety.

Bergmann, ever the pragmatist, attempted to rationalize what she was hearing, to consider the possibilities and to come to some logical explanation for what she was hearing. *What did he mean in saying he'd been expecting us?* To her growing consternation, however, she could think of no answer, no explanation. But she did have the presence of mind to activate the Sol Orbiter One's recording system to capture the exchange taking place below.

Booth, try as he might, could not concoct a plausible theory of how an alien being could shift from one language to another so effortlessly. *They must have some advanced radio technology we haven't even dreamed about that allows them to monitor us.*

Each of the four aboard Sol Orbiter One feared their three fellow crew members might be in imminent danger. And their fears were only exacerbated by the knowledge that they were helpless to intervene.

10

The media were not the only ones concerned with the mounting evidence of mental and emotional instability of Andrus Blount. Totally unfamiliar with diplomacy, he quickly found the strain of being president mentally crushing. His oversensitivity to criticism was amplified many-fold on the international stage and he responded poorly. To every criticism, he answered in kind, taking to twitter to belittle, mock, and attack detractors whom he added to his ever-growing enemies list. To those who dared point out inconsistencies in his public utterances, or to challenge his outright lies, he exploded verbally and on social media. No slight was too small to warrant a response.

"Maybe it's time we reconsidered this 'free press' that we have taken for a constitutional right," he said at one rally, producing a boisterous round of cheers from a crowd carefully culled of all but the most ardent supporters. "Perhaps it's time to take down those people who would question the patriotism of our police," he said, even as heavily armed riot police scanned the crowd for any stray anti-American militants who may have slipped past security.

"Why do we tolerate treasonous activity from those who continue to criticize our military?" he screamed at his rallies. "Our troops are putting their lives on the line to protect democracy in the four corners of the world," he said to enthusiastic cheering and applause from his supporters. Left unsaid was the uncomfortable fact that the U.S. invaded countries that posed no threat to America because they possessed natural resources that could enrich companies controlled by Blount and his corporate supporters. Also not mentioned was Blount's own six medical deferments during the Vietnam War. Bad knees, it was said then, prevented him from serving in the military though more than forty years later, his knees appeared to give him no problems on his many golf courses.

"Why should our corporations, who create jobs for Americans, be penalized by a burdensome tax rate that stifles job growth and sends jobs overseas," he thundered as more and more companies rushed to stash assets in offshore tax havens all the while paying their executives tens of millions in salaries, stock options, and retirement benefits. Middle-class Americans, meanwhile, continued to strive to make it from paycheck to paycheck, coping with increased costs in healthcare, college tuition, and consumer goods.

"Why should our financial institutions be strapped by paralyzing regulations that stymie investment and economic growth?" he bellowed. The crowds cheered and hooted even as Wall Street shed the safeguards that had been put in place, freeing them to renew their reckless speculation in housing, hedge funds, and doomed loans that brought the collapse of 2008. The stock market reacted favorably, climbing to unprecedent heights, ensuring the inevitable fall would be quick, steep, and devastating when it did occur.

No one but the skeptics paid heed but those number were growing daily. When mental health professionals went public with their concerns, Blount reacted with predictable volatility—and classic denial—which served only to galvanize their stated concern. *Malignant narcissism* became the watchword of psychiatrists whose ranks grew in number with each passing day. Malignant narcissism, they said in a single voice, is far more severe than simple narcissism. The latter is a trait shared, to some extent, by virtually all humans. The malignant narcissist, on the other hand, will exhibit symptoms of anti-social behavior where there is a total absence of empathy for others and a complete detachment from reality. That person will display paranoid traits and sadism, and is closely identified with the likes of Idi Amin, Hitler, Stalin, and Trujillo. In short, malignant narcissism is defined as a psychiatric disorder that makes one evil.

And though there was a growing undercurrent of doubt and even overt opposition to Blount and his agenda that sank his approval ratings among Americans, there was little Congress was willing to do to rein him in. The separation of powers doctrine was adhered to, mostly out of fear of becoming the next Blount target. The concept of checks and balances, whereby the judicial, administrative and legislative branches of government each could hold the others accountable was, for all intents and purposes, non-existent as Blount continued to trample on the Constitutional rights of minorities, gays, women, and anyone who dared question his infallibility.

Late night television talk show hosts, who historically had devoted their monologs to stand-up comedy, now took on a more somber critique of Blount's every move, his every tweet, his every public statement. And even though the studio crowds were in general accord with the hosts, Blount immediately took to Twitter to lump then all together as "losers," the preferred label for his critics.

andrusblount@Verified *account*@POTUS.com: *Watched talk shows. Hosts not as funny as they think. Sad, not funny. Could use me as host. I would get lots of laughs. Better ratings!!*

The local municipal and campus police departments, meanwhile, continued to stockpile their departments with military armaments, thanks to Blount's largesse. Their loyalty was being bought and they didn't even know it or if they did, they refused to acknowledge the fact. The harassment of students, especially minorities, was quietly—and effectively— amped up.

Military personnel inexplicably began to appear on patrols of high-crime areas in the larger urban areas. No explanation was given to those who questioned their presence. When reporters did summon the courage to ask why at White House briefings, those inquiries were brushed aside with vague responses of "national security." No further explanations were forthcoming.

Internet service providers were quietly served with court orders that allowed the government to conduct surveillance of online usage of millions of Americans, all without their knowledge or consent. *Facebook* became a fertile ground for profiling. Likewise, federal tax returns of dissidents and other perceived "enemies" were scrutinized by the special investigative agency created by Blount, answerable only to him.

And though the internet and tax snooping were supposed to be top secret, word of the government's invasion of privacy was bound to leak out, and it did, to shrill protests of those who began to find themselves pulled over in unexplained traffic stops, searches, and detentions, all with no warrants and with no opportunity to engage legal counsel. Illegal drugs were conveniently "found" in unauthorized searches of homes and vehicles belonging to dissidents as civil liberties quickly became but a fond memory of what once was.

11

The stranger alit from his scrawny horse and extended his hand and I stared at it with more than a little apprehension for perhaps a beat too long. "The name's Johansson, Lars Johansson," he said. His warm smile somehow conveyed to me that he was not a threat to us.

"Colonel Travis Whitten," I responded, taking the man's hand. "Is that Swedish?" I asked and immediately regretted asking such a question on an alien planet. His answer surprised me.

"Yes, it is," Johansson said. "Strangely enough, our continents, nationalities and languages on Terranum are the same as yours. At one time, our civilization was a couple of centuries ahead of yours. Our challenges, believe it or not, were the same, but I'm afraid we're long past setting the standards for advancement."

"Challenges?" I repeated. We were already walking in what felt like a southerly direction with Vasquez and Nguyen following closely behind, their minds spinning over their host's obvious familiarity with the backgrounds of these visitors he'd met only minutes before. As we walked, my mind was racing. I'd heard the term Terranum somewhere before but he couldn't remember where or when. The word gnawed at him as if he was experiencing *déjà vu*.

"We'll explain all that when we get to the village," Johansson said, smiling. Despite the loss of one eye and his apparent lack of proper nourishment, he appeared to be in fair health, about fifty or sixty years of age. Maybe older, maybe younger; it was difficult to tell. His hair, graying about the temples, was thinning on top and his deeply tanned face was etched with lines and wrinkles. He stood a little less than six feet but appeared taller because he was so thin and bony. His pants, ragged as they were, were short, not even covering his ankles which, like his feet, were bare. His fingernails were long and dirty. "Did you have a nice trip?" He asked the question as if he were asking about a drive of a couple of hundred miles over a few hours instead of a two-month space mission covering more than forty million miles.

"No problems until we spotted you," I said, not knowing how exactly to answer. "We thought we'd encountered Earth but obviously not. We can't wait to learn more about you."

"Well, we already know about you and we'll tell you everything you want to know about us. We have important information to give you to take back to Earth."

The realization began to sink in with all three of us that this man was intimately knowledgeable about us and our home and that his knowledge was more detailed than we could imagine. *But how? How could he possibly know about us?*

We had walked more than half-a-mile when, about six hundred yards beyond the dead trees, we could detect movement. As the four of us got closer, we could make out the figures of about seventy or eighty people milling around as if waiting for our arrival, which, it turned out, they were.

Johansson was apparently an emissary sent out to greet the visitors. He seemed to read our innermost thoughts. "I came alone because we were concerned that if we all came, you might assume we were hostile. I can assure you, we are not."

"Are you the leader?" I asked.

"We don't have leaders in the sense you understand the term. We once did, but now we are a cooperative, each contributing his or her share toward the overall benefit of the village as a whole. That is how we survive after the wars. All that will be explained, but first we eat. By the way, you can remove your suits, or at least your helmets. We have the same oxygen that you breathe on Earth, and our climate is identical to your own."

As commander, I it was my duty to set the example for the others, so I slowly loosened my helmet and removed it, careful to shut off the oxygen supply from my tank before doing so. When the helmet was removed, I inhaled deeply and nodded to the others who then began to undo their own headgear.

"How long do you have here before your shuttle pilot follows your orders to continue on without you?"

"Two days," I answer, my wonder at his host's perception growing with each new observation. I immediately regretted any admission before learning more about our hosts.

"Your radio batteries are solar-powered, I presume," Johansson said.

"Affirmative."

"Excellent. You'll want to keep the lines of communication open with your shuttle. What do you call it?"

"Sol Orbiter One."

"Ah, quite appropriate. Much better than Apollo or Saturn."

The easy, almost cavalier reference to NASA's Apollo and Saturn missions stunned us on the ground as well as our crew mates aboard Sol Orbiter One. "What the hell....?" Stammered Vasquez.

Johansson laughed aloud. "All in good time, young man, all in good time."

12

There was little question in retrospect that fear and anxiety on the part of the American electorate propelled an opportunist like Blount, fully prepared and willing to exploit those emotions, into the presidency. That was evident enough during the acrimonious campaign. But now, those same feelings gripped world leaders, diplomats and media the world over as well. He was wholly unprepared for the job and could only rule by arousing feelings of his followers through appeals to bigotry, racism, and militarism. This he did effectively through his base of evangelicals and Second Amendment fanatics who raved against abortion but could see no reason to change gun laws to protect innocent school children from mass murderers. Life was precious, but only on their narrow terms.

And even as his supporters defended the Bill of Rights as some sort of Biblical commandment from on high insofar as it upheld Second Amendment gun rights, they disparaged any such rights under the First Amendment as it pertained to freedom of the press. Following Blount's lead, his followers echoed his claims that the press was "the enemy of the people." Paradoxically, they saw no inconsistency in holding one amendment, the Second, as sacred while condemning another, the First, to Blount's catch-all "fake news" status.

His rock-solid base was referred to as the thirty-five percenters, so called for his consistent approval ratings which languished in the thirty-five percent range. That, number apparently was sufficient to intimidate members of Blount's party in Congress to go along with his legislative agenda even if everything he proposed was to the disadvantage of that very base. Those were the rednecks and uneducated middle- to low-income bulk of Americans who continued to be fooled by duplicitous politicians who insisted they were working in their interests.

Now that he had been in office for nearly a year, the media were becoming more and more critical of his every move, his every utterance, his every post on Twitter. And with increasing frequency, international human rights organizations, domestic civil rights groups, LGBGT advocates, prisoner rights organizations, and civil libertarians clashed in demonstrations with Blount supporters. Those supporters were invariably neo-Nazis white supremacists, anti-Semitics, anti-Muslims, anti-Mexican, pro-gun-rights advocates, and ignorant rednecks whose fears Blount exploited as expertly as any seasoned politician. He knew how to rally a crowd to take out the occasional protester at his rallies. Gun-toting and club-wielding thugs regularly waded into peace protesters in city after city. Whenever there was violence, Blount would take to Twitter to condemn the protesters and to encourage even more violence.

Between his new secret police agency answerable only to him and municipal and campus police armed to the teeth, peaceful protesters stood little chance to make their voices heard. Students, professors, lawyers, and anyone else who dared speak up in public were quickly subjected to unconstitutional stops, searches and imprisonment, all in the name of national security.

As the media ramped up its condemnation of the administration's violation of basic rights, Blount's forces retaliated by applying more pressure on corporations to pull advertising from the networks and newspapers. To refuse subjected corporations to intensive tax audits and federal grand jury investigations. Unspoken was the looming threat of the loss of generous tax exemptions. Companies got the message and the media quickly felt the heat in the form of revenue loss. Not only were the media strongly encouraged to pull back on criticisms of Blount, but subtle intimidation even convinced some newspapers and news services to begin churning out pro-Blount propaganda. The last line of defense to despotic rule was beginning to crumble.

As Blount grew more and more powerful and as his constitutional abuses more and more severe, the reactions were somewhat mixed. On the one hand, a timid Congress cowered in his wake, afraid to confront him, especially the members from within his own party. Even as he heaped insults on individual members of his party in both the House and Senate, they continued to praise his agenda publicly, all the while wondering privately what could be done to rein him in. Never mind that for years his party had been rolling out a political strategy that created the monster with which they now tried to contend.

The party had for decades been trying to stack the Supreme Court. It had gerrymandered congressional districts to nullify African-American representation, and to suppress voter registration among Blacks and Hispanics and to a lesser extent, women. Efforts to enact guarantees of equal rights for women and gays were regularly killed in committee. Women, despite efforts on their behalf, continued to earn only sixty cents to every dollar their male counterparts made. For black women, the disparity was even greater.

Similar efforts by his party extended into the fifty state houses with bills to cut funding for social programs, programs for the arts, public education, higher education, health care, care for the mentally ill, and even care for homeless veterans. Instead of implementing rehabilitation programs for minor offenders, stiffer penalties were enacted which resulted in more offenders, mostly minorities, being sent to prisons while white collar criminals, especially those who headed up hedge funds and Wall Street banks that stole billions went unpunished. Punishment, if there was any, was in the form of fines which were (a) less than the amounts stolen by the white-collar criminals and (b) invariably paid by the companies' shareholders and not the actual perpetrators.

As prisons became more and more overcrowded with the minor offenders and illegal immigrants rounded up by Blount's enforcers, the need grew for jail space. Thus, the private prison industry, already a thriving enterprise, grew exponentially. Those private prisons, which were already paid well to serve as human warehouses, quickly learned there was much more money to be made by hiring out prisoners to companies in the form of work release. Prisoners were generally paid only minimum wage and even at that, were required to pony up sixty percent of their wages to the prisons. The institutions profiteered even further by running concession stands where they got the remainder of their earnings by gouging prisoners on the prices of soft drinks and snacks. And when they got all the prisoners' money, there was always money to be extracted from inmates' families via private telephone services which charged exorbitant prices for collect calls home by prisoners. It was a business plan straight from the Blount playbook.

And the executives of those private prisons knew how to keep the money coming in by simply investing a few thousand dollars in key political campaigns. Blount and his lap dogs in Congress and those in the state legislatures similarly predisposed to currying favor with this pseudo-populist saw nothing wrong with the way they were funneling the least threatening offenders into a system to be exploited in such a manner.

Everyone was happy. Or so it seemed. But there was a growing undercurrent of discontent and it was quietly gaining momentum every day. Blount, even in his diminished mental capacity which, now deteriorating more with each passing day, somehow realized this and knew he needed something to bolster his poll numbers in order to reinforce his power.

He needed a war. And if there was a good war, there would be a national emergency that in turn would justify suspending all elections so that he could assume the status of permanent Commander in Chief.

13

We couldn't help noticing the sparse vegetation but the near total absence of birds and small animals failed to register with us at first. But we were aghast the moment we observed the physical appearance of the natives of this scorched planet. Their emaciated, haggard features grabbed our attention immediately. Lars Johansson, with his gnarly physique and one good eye, was strange enough. But the people who gathered around us now were positively grotesque. Many had burns covering their bodies. Others, even the women, had only splotches of hair on their heads. A few had hideous tumors on their skin. Some were completely blind. Only the youngest appeared to have normal features, and there were precious few under the age of sixty, or so it appeared.

There were, it turned out, about thirty in the party sent out to meet Lars and his curious guests and to provide escort into the village which was still nearly a mile away. The village itself consisted of crude huts thrown together from scraps of lumber, logs, charred bricks and cinderblocks, and whatever else could be scrounged from the ruins of a once-superior civilization. The village was a beehive of activity as more than a thousand residents busied themselves in attempts to make their visitors welcome. Before entering the primitive settlement, we detected the aroma of food.

"We're preparing a meal for you," Johansson said. "There is a critical scarcity of vegetables and red meat, but we have plenty of nourishment from the sea. We are but one of many such settlements along the Atlantic, Pacific and Gulf coasts, major rivers, and the shorelines of the Great Lakes. We rely on the sea and lakes to provide our food. Everything else has been destroyed.

"Our population was once more than three hundred fifty million. We are now fewer than two million and we're scattered across the country. As far as we can tell, this is one of the larger camps. Our world population once exceeded eight billion. That was only ten years ago. We don't really know what it is now, but our best guess is somewhere between sixty million and a hundred million."

"What happened?" I asked, baffled. "Pandemic, famine, war?"

"War first. Then famine and pandemic. But patience. All your questions will be answered after we eat."

More and more people fell in behind us as we entered the village. To us, who had not eaten solid food in two months, the smell of the seafood being cooked, whatever it was, was inviting and overpowering. We could wait for the stories. For now, there was meal to be eaten and the looks on the faces of our hosts was that of sincere welcome for an old friend or family member they had been expecting for some time. It was impossible for us to fully understand, but for whatever reason, we began to share the feeling that we were home. The prospect of real food may have influenced our thinking. Or perhaps it was the congeniality of our hosts. Whatever it was, for the first time since the LEM had set down on this struggling planet called Terranum, we allowed ourselves to relax.

14

Dr. Frederick Feinberg reached a decision from which he knew there would be no turning back. For some time now, he had been concerned over the erratic behavior of Andrus Blount. Finally, he had seen enough. The President was out of control. His non-stop tweets were both self-serving and unreasoned rants. His insulting of world leaders long considered allies stood in sharp contrast to his coziness with tyrannical dictators who routinely slaughtered their own people. And his constant reversals of stated policy screamed of a delusional disorder known as psychopathy, also sometimes called sociopathy.

German psychologist and psychoanalyst Erich Fromm, who fled Nazi Germany, had another name for the disorder: malignant narcissism, a condition he described as "the quintessence of evil" long before the world ever heard of Andrus Blount. Feinberg could find no reason to dispute Fromm's definition, nor could he dispute the conviction that Blount displayed the most dangerous symptoms of pathological narcissism.

Thomas Jefferson stressed the importance of an informed citizenry as the best protection for democracy. But Feinberg and his colleagues were in a catch-22 position. On the one hand, they felt an obligation to inform the country of the dangers presented by Blount's obvious mental deficiencies. On the other, they were bound by a doctrine adopted by the Goldwater rule.

The Goldwater rule came into being after a group of psychiatrists diagnosed Barry Goldwater, the 1964 Republican candidate for President, as paranoid schizophrenic when he advocated the use of nuclear weapons in the Cold War with the Soviet Union. Goldwater successfully sued a magazine in which the psychiatrist poll was published which in turned prompted the American Psychiatric Association to adopt the rule, which said it was unethical for psychiatrists to diagnose, or even comment on, a public figure unless there was an actual examination.

Compounding Jefferson's advocacy of a free and unfettered press was Blount's non-stop attacks on the news media. Any story that did not comort with his version of the truth was immediately branded as bogus and biased or, to use his favorite term, "fake news." His political base pounced on his denunciations of the media, eager to validate his rants. Reporters were physically attacked and beaten with little intervention by police. More than once, it was Blount's protection detail, drawn from his newly-formed secret police and not the Secret Service, that initiated the attacks on reporters.

Feinberg began discretely reaching out to his peers whom he knew to be equally concerned about Blount's spiraling mental state. Initially, there were seven whom he contacted. But each of those seven knew other psychiatrists who shared their fears. Within a matter of a few weeks, a furtive meeting was called. Sworn to utmost secrecy, seventy-one psychiatrists descended on Kansas City for what ostensibly was a routine conference of mental health professionals. In reality, the attendees were there to lay the groundwork for a comprehensive informational campaign to educate America—and the world—of the perilous course on which Andrus Blount had set the nation and of his fragile mental condition that placed the world on the brink of nuclear annihilation.

Security for the conference was airtight. Credentials of attendees were checked, and triple-checked. Cell phones were confiscated, to be returned following the session. The meeting was held in a hotel near Kansas City International Airport. The meeting room was sealed off and guarded by a private security firm. Wait staff served meals but were barred from the meeting room once the meal was finished and the business session started. Thomas Jefferson's words notwithstanding, reporters were likewise banished. There could be absolutely no leaks before the group's plan was implemented. No head of state had ever received more protection than the seventy-one mental health professionals in that incubator meeting.

After the distinguished psychiatrists finished their meals and the wait staff had been escorted from the room, Dr. Frederick Feinberg stood and walked to the dais. "Ladies and gentlemen, thank you for coming her

74

today for this critical planning session. I trust you all are prepared for the consequences of what we are about to undertake. I would ask that you not take notes."

15

We were careful about consuming solid food after two months of the formula diet developed especially by NASA for in-flight nutrition, so we only picked at the meal we were fed by our hosts. Afterwards, the three of us settled in to hear the story of this strange new land and these people who knew so much about us. Sitting opposite us at the roughhewn table were Lars Johansson and two other residents of the primitive village. The first introduced himself as James Underwood. I estimated him to be about sixty, though he looked much older. Under the conditions these people found themselves, who could tell? He had no teeth and, like Lars, his skin hung on a gaunt frame that was tanned deep brown. His bright blue eyes, however, revealed a man whose senses were still as sharp as those of a man a twenty- or thirty-years younger. His movements were spry and his muscles appeared strong despite his skinny frame.

A woman, also perhaps sixty, sat to his left. She was short and while somewhat heavier than most of the other women in the camp, was nonetheless conditioned to the rigors of her living conditions. She had set about clearing the table after the meal was finished without asking assistance from the men, who carried out their own chores of burying the leftover food and table scraps so as not to attract rodents and insects. Her name was Meredith Sanders. She was a widow, she explained who had lost her husband in the war. Like everyone else, she had joined the village out of necessity and now was a part of the clan in which every person pulled his or her own weight.

Following the introductions, Lars opened the discussion. "Where would like us to begin?" he asked.

"Well, it would be interesting to know how you obtained so much knowledge about us and our society," I said, setting my drink down.

"That's easy," Lars said. "Apparently, we are anywhere from ten to forty or fifty years, to an entire century ahead of you in development, depending on what area of development you're talking about—or at least we were." His voice trailed off as he added the last phrase.

"We embarked on a mission just like yours about one hundred fifty years ago," he said. "Like you, we had no idea there was another planet in our same orbital path, a planet with identical living conditions, but decades behind us. We found you just as you found us, by mistake. And like you, we landed. Unlike you, we were undetected because you lacked the sophisticated detection equipment you now take for granted."

"What did you do when you found us?" asked Whitten "Obviously, you didn't introduce yourselves."

"We knew that we couldn't. You would've had us committed—or executed. You had just begun moving toward your Civil War, so we spared you the trauma of dealing with alien visitors. We simply assimilated into your society. It was an easy matter for us. We had the computer technology that you are only now acquiring and using—and you still have many more developments to make in that area provided you don't destroy yourselves first as we did. We continued sending missions—and people—to earth. We watched as you experienced presidential assassinations. We continued observing as you moved into World War I and your Great Depression and World War II.

As you progressed, we had to make adjustments to blend in. To hack into the social security system in America, for example, was a simple process that allowed us to become working citizens in your country literally overnight. We would wait a few months and apply for a 'duplicate' social security card, explaining that ours had been lost. And as more missions were sent out, we settled in other countries to observe and learn their languages and their ways."

Lars stopped to light a pipe. "Smoking, unfortunately, we learned from you."

"Did you participate in government, intervene in helping to shape events?"

"Only in the most mischievous of ways. As I said, we were there to observe only. But a couple of our people got caught up in your addiction to sports. Do you remember Super Bowl III in January of 1969 when the Jets upset the Colts? Or the '69 Mets beating the Orioles? Those weren't the big upsets that you may think. No way were the Jets better than the Colts without a little help. And those catches Tommy Agee made against the Orioles? You think he barely got to the balls but he was destined to make those catches, no matter what. And Baltimore was the victim both times."

"Wait," I interrupted. "You arranged those? How? What about that catch Willie Mays made in the '54 World Series? And Bobby Thompson's home run in '51? Was that more 'mischief?'"

"Well, you certainly know your baseball history. But no, that was all Willie Mays and Bobby Thompson," Lars said, laughing. "It was just in '69. Apparently, the perpetrators had some kind of personal grudge against Baltimore and when we found out what they had done, we dispatched them home. As for the 'how,' that's one of the developments yet to be made by you. It involves the power of mind over matter."

I laughed as I shook my head at his admission. "I've heard of that, but I thought it was just a lot of hooey."

"No, it's very real. And remember, we were centuries ahead of you in other advances as well."

"Like what?" I asked.

"Medicine, for one. We had a cure for cancer before our wars destroyed all our technology. We developed microchips, automobiles, airplanes, lasers, fiber optics, space flight, and of course, nuclear warfare, to name just a few."

There was an obvious question I had to ask. "Couldn't you have introduced your technological advances without blowing your cover? I mean, a cure for cancer?"

"You couldn't even treat a cut properly without giving patients staph infections. It wasn't until the mid-nineteenth century that a doctor finally came up with the notion that washing hands after treating a patient might be a good idea. And what happened when he went public with his theory? He was ridiculed.

"You still had eight-party phone lines long after we were using cell phones almost exclusively." You simply weren't ready for the introduction of such revolutionary advances. We did introduce some new things but we had to do it very gradually and deliberately because your infrastructure couldn't support automobiles, cell phones, laser surgery, and certainly not computers if we suddenly dumped all those in hour lap."

How long did you observe us?" asked Nguyen Huy who, up until now had been content to listen.

"We never stopped. We have people there now—nearly five million, in fact. Of course, now that our civilization and our space program have been destroyed, they're stranded there. They're your citizens now. Another thirty million are in every other advanced country on Earth and if you work with them, you can still save your planet before it's too late."

We could only stare at him in silence, not knowing exactly what questions to ask but too intrigued not to ask something. Finally, Vasquez, the youngest one there, managed to speak. "What are we supposed to save ourselves from? Is there some kind of interplanetary war coming?"

Lars took a long pull on his pipe and exhaled the rich, blue smoke before answering in a low deliberate tone. "There is a war coming. It won't be interplanetary but will be worse than anything you could imagine unless you act to change the course of history."

****

High above, in Sol Orbiter One, Wilhite, Patel, Bergmann, and Booth listened to the exchange, transfixed, as if afraid to move lest they miss some crucial bit of dialog. The sense of apprehension that coursed through their veins was palatable in the craft. A combined fear for their comrades' safety and overwhelming curiosity about what stories Johansson, Underwood, and Sanders were about to reveal to the three on the ground. Somehow, they sensed they were about to hear stories they never dared to imagine. Bergmann, certain of that, switched on a second digital recorder as a back-up because, as much as anything, she just didn't know what else to do.

No one spoke though each was keenly aware they had only eighteen hours before Nguyen, Vasquez, and I either returned to Sol Orbiter One or the remaining four continued on to their rendezvous with Earth without them. No consideration had yet been given to how they would explain the loss of three of their fellow crew members when—and if—they got home.

16

"**I** don't suppose it is necessary that I reiterate the reason we are all here," Dr. Frederick Feinberg began. "I assume we all share the same deep concerns but just in case there might be any misunderstanding, if there is anyone here who is not prepared to take a public stand on the issue of President Andrus Blount's mental capacity as President of the United States, I would ask that you excuse yourself at this time."

He paused and looked out over the audience of his peers. Not one person among them moved. They were, if this is appropriate to say of a group of psychiatrists, of one mind.

"The last thing any of us wanted was to find it necessary to convene here today for the purpose on which we are about to embark," he said after ascertaining there were no defectors among the attendees. "I'm not going to insult your intelligence by defining all the types of mental illnesses that define President Blount's behavior. Suffice it to say we all have already arrived at our conclusions or we wouldn't be here. The question then, is what are we going to do about it? What *can* we do about it?"

He devoted the next fifty minutes itemizing various inconsistent and contradictory statements and actions of Blount without bothering to try and diagnose his mental state. That, after all, had been done in the minds of everyone present well before the meeting was convened. But by listing all the utterances, all the tweets, all the pandering to his base, all the incongruities, he underscored the urgency of their assembled purpose.

"The American Psychiatric Association adopted the so-called 'Goldwater rule' after the 1964 election that prevented professionals in our field from commenting on the mental stability of our leaders without an actual examination of the individual. Of course, had we been able to conduct an examination, we were prevented from commenting because of patient-doctor confidentiality restrictions, so what're you gonna do?"

That elicited chuckles from around the room. "That 'Goldwater rule' prevented us from speaking out when Richard Nixon retreated into the darkness of his own mind. We didn't speak up when he bombed Cambodia. We were mute when the evils of the Watergate scandal were unveiled and we continued our silence when we could all see President Reagan, our personal feelings about him notwithstanding, slowly slipping away.

"But our silence has not only been with our own leaders. No one in our profession uttered a word about the madness of Hitler or Idi Amin. Where were we when Bashar al-Assad and Saddam Hussein were slaughtering hundreds of thousands of their own people?

"President Blount has castigated the press which is already crippled by the Internet. President Blount has formed his own news network and his own secret police, much in the same manner of Hitler. Reporters are too timid to speak out because of threats to bar them from press briefings, or worse. Our law enforcement agencies have had their loyalty purchased with military armaments, armaments meant to be used on American citizens who dare disagree with official policy or actions. And now President Blount is rattling the sabers of nuclear war, a war in which there can be no victors but only survivors. If our own members of Congress refuse to speak up because of some blind loyalty to one political party or the other over common sense, then who will?

"I submit to you, my fellow experts in the field of mental health, that we have not only the expertise to expose the dangerous irrationality of this mad tyrant, but a duty to do so, as well."

A hand went up from the middle of the room. "Yes, Dr. Dierdorff?" Feinberg said, recognizing an eminent psychiatrist from Boston.

"What *can* we do if we are bound by 'Goldwater'?"

Feinberg paused to let the gravity of his response sink in. "We may have no alternative but to withdraw from the American Psychiatric Association if the APA does not back us up on this. We may have to form our own association. If it comes to that, it would be my hope that more psychiatrists will join us to give us strength in numbers."

Another hand and a voice saying, "What do you propose as our course of action?

"That was Dr. Rubin Sloan from San Francisco in case you didn't see who asked that question," Feinberg said. "Dr. Sloan, the only thing we *can* do is to launch a major public relations campaign, the kind of thing the politicians do to get elected. Maybe even retain the services of a lobbying firm."

"You mean lie through our teeth?" came a voice from the back. The room erupted with laughter.

"And they say we psychiatrists don't have a sense of humor," Feinberg shot back. "To answer your question, which I trust was in jest, no, we do just the opposite. We tell the hard, naked truth and wait for the fecal matter to hit the oscillating air manipulation device."

"The *what*?"

"The shit to hit the fan." More laughter. "Seriously, we can expect some major push back from the APA perhaps, definitely from President Blount supporters and a major assault from President Blount and his attack dogs. Knowing the way President Blount thinks, we can probably anticipate threatened legal action in a variety of forms. But I think court action would probably be a big mistake on Blount's part. A lawsuit would ensure we had a national forum from which to deliver our message, courtesy of President Blount himself."

"What kind of public relations campaign are you talking about?" another asked.

"I would ask that you please be recognized before yelling out your questions," Feinberg said. "That's the only way we can get through this. To answer your question, it's going to take a massive television and print media advertising campaign as well as social media and it's going to be expensive. We need to set up a political action committee and a Web site to solicit contributions. It's going to take millions of dollars to pull this off."

A hand shot up. "Doesn't the APA already have a PAC?" asked Dr. Ted Winfield of Chicago.

"Yes, but I don't think APA will allow us to use funds from its PAC for this purpose. We're going to have to form a separate organization."

"Then let's do it!" someone shouted.

"Are you willing to put that in the form of a motion?" Feinberg asked.

"I so move!" yelled Dr. Ray Bordelon of New Orleans.

"Second!" came the call from several voices simultaneously.

"I'll give the second to Dr. Winfield since I was looking at him. All in favor?"

By unanimous vote the Political Action Committee was approved.

"I think we got this a little backward," said Feinberg. We don't have a name for our organization yet."

"I move for the formal creation of the Association of Patriotic Psychiatrists."

"Do I have a second?"

"Second!"

"All in favor?"

Again, the vote was unanimous.

The only order of business left was the election of officers and a board of directors. Feinberg was chosen as the new group's president by acclamation and Ted Winfield was chosen vice president. Dr. Robert Gorman of Philadelphia was elected secretary and Dr. James Steinmann of Orlando was chosen as treasurer. Twelve board members representing a cross section of the U.S. were chosen and Dr. Jules Wattley was elected chairman. All actions taken by the new association would require two-thirds approval of the board, according to by-laws yet to be drawn up. Once written, approval of a simple majority of the entire membership would be required.

In less than four hours, the course was set on a plan from which there would be no turning back. Despite the unanimity, there was little to celebrate. They left the meeting with faces drawn from tension but with a common sense of purpose: to save the country from a madman.

17

"What kind of war?" I asked as I finished my drink.

"I'll get to that," Lars said. "But first you need to know more about us.

"As I said before, we once were hundreds of years ahead of your Earth in our development. We had computers more than a century ago that were probably superior even then to what you have today. You were well into your Internet and social media when our last mission returned from your Earth about ten years ago. We had our influenza pandemic precisely like yours in 1918, only a century before. We had our world wars and our own assassinations, just as you did. We knew in advance that President Kennedy, Martin Luther King and Robert Kennedy would be killed because we went through the same agonizing period in our own history. The only thing different were the names. We knew the Vietnam War would tear your country apart—and it did, just as it did with us. We knew Watergate would occur. Everything you experienced, we suffered through years and years before. It's like your movie *Groundhog Day*."

"Why didn't you try to warn us?"

"We couldn't. First of all, I've already told you we were there only to observe. Second, who would've believed us? Would you have believed someone who approached you and said he was from another planet and he wanted to avert a disaster? Third, we didn't know the precise dates in advance—only a general timeframe of when each event would happen."

"Point taken. But if you knew all those things, do you know who killed Kennedy?"

Lars squinted at Whitten through the smoke that wafted from his pipe. "It wasn't who the Warren Commission said, if that's what you're driving at. It wasn't Oswald. Oh, he was there in the book depository and he had a rifle. He'd brought it to work because a co-worker said he wanted to buy it from him. The co-worker never showed up and Oswald took the fall just as planned."

"Who was the killer?"

"You mean killers plural, don't you? And it's for the best that you not know. The Warren Commission knew but they also knew what would've happened if they'd told the truth. We were there and we monitored everything: Dallas, New Orleans, Cuba, Miami, Washington. I can tell you there was a direct link between what happened in Dallas and what happened at the Watergate Office Building nine years later."

I felt a sudden chill run through my body as we he listened to Johansson relate how the citizens of Earth had been spied on for nearly two centuries. Without a word passing between the three of us, we shared a feeling of intrigue. At the same time, we were offended that every action taken, every word uttered by citizens in the Americas, Europe, Asia, and Africa—probably every nation the world over—had been monitored by people walking among them who knew what disasters and what promises lay ahead but were unable—or unwilling—to speak out.

Lars continued after again lighting his pipe and puffing vigorously to get the tobacco burning. "We survived our own First World War and came out of it stronger than ever. Likewise, our Second World War. So, we knew you, too, would emerge stronger and more prosperous.

"Your Eisenhower warned about the undue influence of the military-industrial complex. We heard that same warning sixty years before and like you, we paid no heed. And like you, we saw a complete takeover of our political system by military contractors, big banks, pharmaceutical companies, and the petroleum industry. Our citizens lost their political voices just as yours have lost theirs in recent years."

He paused to survey his guests. Our eyes were locked on his as we listened to his words. Neither of us had any inclination to interrupt with questions now. We were rapt at what he was telling us. I hoped everything Johansson was saying was being recorded aboard the Sol Orbiter One.

He went on. "Slowly at first, and then it seems, almost overnight, our Congress lost its political balance as one party began to dominate over the other. That was the party that was receiving all the corporate campaign funds from the corporations and their lobbyists. Candidates ran for office from the dominant party with patriotic and religious slogans that resonated with the uneducated among their supporters. Then their messages became shriller, more vitriolic, attacking those with ideas and philosophies that differed with their own. This, of course, only fed the flames of hatred that the party was spreading as the centerpiece of its strategy to divide the country."

"What party are you talking about?" I forced myself to ask.

"Do I really need to tell you that?" Johansson answered with a grin and raised eyebrows before continuing.

"They had a proposed program that they planned to implement if their party again won the presidency and control of both chambers of Congress. They advocated ending no fault divorce, why we never knew, other than to consign women to a role of subservience and as a means of producing offspring.

"Other objectives in their program included a total ban on abortions with no exceptions, a ban on contraceptives, greater tax breaks for corporations and the rich while increasing the tax burden on the working class; elimination of labor unions, child labor laws and worker safety protections while raising the retirement age; cuts to all social programs and medical care; raising prescription drug prices; eliminating the education department while allocating public funds for religious schools; requiring religious beliefs to be taught in all schools; rolling back all previous civil rights gains while prohibiting the teaching about slavery and of civil rights and gender studies in schools; ending climate protection; ending all corporate regulations, promoting and increasing capital punishment, ending marriage equality, condemning single mothers while promoting the so-called 'traditional family'; using the military to break up domestic civil protests; increasing the deportation of non-citizens and incarcerations; elimination of federal agencies and continuing to pack our Supreme Court and federal courts with judges adhering to their political agenda."

Lars continued with his description of the proposals that had been proposed as a platform in his country's election. "They called for the elimination of early childhood education with the full knowledge that it would have a disastrous economic impact on low-income families. They wanted to dismantle the federal education department and to gut funding for public education by supporting vouchers that would funnel the money to private school tuitions – all while phasing out funding for the low-income schools.

"The religious arm of the party, which in truth, controlled every aspect of the party, wanted to abolish all rights gained by women, including their rights in reproductive decisions, employment and even voting, rights which had taken decades and decades of struggle to obtain. They even said that women's rights to contraceptives should be taken from them and that abortion should be outlawed, even in cases of rape and incest. Yet, even while defending a child's right to life, even from the moment of conception, they turned their collective backs on the children the moment they were born.

"We had Blacks, Asians, Hispanics, gays and Jews who struggled over several lifetimes to achieve equality and acceptance. All that was to be wiped away under the party's proposals. No minority's rights would be recognized under the plan.

"Federal employees who had spent their entire careers in low-paying civil service jobs were told they were expendable. Tens of thousands of public employees would lose their jobs under the plan. Gone were the protections that had been enacted to protect their jobs from political influence.

"More and bigger tax breaks were proposed for corporations and the wealthiest of the wealthy while more and greater tax burdens were to be imposed upon the working class. To further add to the hardships of the middle class and low-income families, a national sales tax was pushed hard. I don't have to tell you that paying a five- or ten-percent tax on everything you purchase is much harder on someone who is already barely getting by as opposed to someone who lives in the lap of luxury.

"Yeah," I managed to say. "That's pretty obvious."

Lars didn't even acknowledge my agreement. He continued his description of the agenda pushed by the party in control.

"They had been screaming about illegal immigration for years and finally, they were in the position to force their plan with their same old scare tactics. The biggest claim was that immigrants were stealing jobs from citizens and that they were paying no taxes. Of course, the only way they could get away with avoiding taxes was if they were working 'off the books,' or for cash. If that were the case, then the employers were every bit as complicit as the workers – but the party conveniently overlooked that pesky fact. Also overlooked was the fact that undocumented workers paid $100 billion in federal, state and local taxes in the year immediately preceding the election. Rather than dwell on that, the advocates turned to manufactured statistics on crime committed by 'illegal immigrants.' Again, they simply ignored that crime was being committed across the spectrum of demographics: race, age and gender and the so-called illegal immigrants were no more nor no less guilty of a high crime rate that in truth, was decreasing – another misrepresentation of the relevant facts.

"And climate change denial was a huge part of their proposal, despite tons of evidence to the contrary. Rather than encouraging a move to environmental-friendly fuel such as wind and solar, they were practically fanatical in their support for more and more drilling for fossil fuel."

Lars paused when he noticed the rest of us staring at each in disbelief.

"That sounds like our Republican Party's Project 2025," I managed to sputter.

"Strange coincidence, no?"

"Did they win and were their policies implemented?"

"Look around you and see for yourself. What do you think? As the giant corporations began to wield more and more influence with their propaganda, they were able to elect candidates who were only too happy to roll back regulations that had protected the citizenry from fraud since our own Great Depression which, by the way, preceded yours by sixty-two years. Freed of the laws and regulations that had kept them honest, they then went after tax 'reforms' that favored the richest among us to the detriment of our middle class. Once in power, judges were appointed who supported their agenda. Sound familiar?

"It was at this time that a tyrant, a billionaire businessman who cheated contractors and stole from people, decided he should be our leader. His name was Randall Modell. At first no one took him seriously. He was a pompous buffoon. But he started to say things that resonated with those who imagined themselves disenfranchised. They had no idea how well they had things but that didn't deter them from hating minorities, immigrants, anyone who didn't look or think as they did. It was xenophobia at its best. The more he ranted and raved at his rallies, the more his supporters frothed at their mouths as they cheered him on. At last, there was a candidate who spoke to them about their concerns and fears.

"The man no one gave a chance to win, won. He immediately set about undoing everything his predecessor had accomplished. Anything that had his name on it was repealed or cancelled by a Modell executive order. Seizing on the fears of his supporters, he went for the kill in rounding up all immigrants, even their children who were born here. It wasn't enough that he simply rounded them up, however. He separated children from parents, wives from husbands—just as had been done with the slaves here and in your country and just as was done by your Hitler and our similar psychopathic criminal who plunged our own world into war.

"All the while, with Modell's encouragement, our congress began passing laws that allowed the rich to continue to get richer while the middle and low-income people, the very ones who elected Modell, bore the burden of taxes and saw their wages frozen—if they even had jobs after the companies began relocating in other countries where the labor was much cheaper and there were no unions."

"I was a union organizer," James Underwood interjected. "But then, they began passing the so-called right-to-work laws that gutted the unions and soon organized labor, which had built this country after our Second World War, had no leverage to bargain for better salaries and benefits. Pension programs were eliminated and health benefits reduced almost to the point of being worthless. Our membership which once boasted tens of millions of workers plummeted. Elected officials who once hung onto our every word and who relied on our support to get elected no longer would even give us the time of day. Overnight we became persona non-grata."

Meredith Sanders leaned forward, her hands clasped together on the table top. "I was a teacher. When I started, it was considered a noble profession, one that garnered instant respect. But then the party began attacking public education and cutting budgets. Soon, they were cutting the budgets of higher education, making it impossible for middle- and low-income families to afford to send their kids to college. We woke up one day to find we were second-class citizens. Public funding had been siphoned off to private and charter schools, schools attended by children of the party leaders and their wealthy campaign donors."

"She's absolutely correct," Johansson said. "our public education system was left in the dust and our state universities overnight became private colleges. Tuition increased tenfold. State-sponsored scholarship programs ostensibly passed to help low-income students instead were directed to upper-income students. Because of the influx of these scholarships, students suddenly had money for more expensive off-campus housing. Speculators started construction of condos and apartment complexes financed through university foundations while low-income students still found themselves forced into community colleges—if they got in a college at all.

"Still, the rhetoric spewed by the party was what the so-called great unwashed wanted to hear: The right to own assault weapons was placed on an altar, valued more than freedom of the press, which was demonized. Minority voters were purged from the rolls and our congressional districts were re-drawn to favor candidates who spoke for the rich. Candidates railed against illegal immigration, special treatment for minorities, social programs for the welfare cheats. The tide of public opinion was slowly but steadily turned by a well-oiled propaganda machine. The few voices of reason that attempted to be heard over the clatter were drowned out.

"It didn't matter that what the corporations were stealing from the system dwarfed anything welfare recipients were getting illegally. Nor did it seem to matter that many of those social programs were aiding the very ones who wanted them abolished. Programs for the arts benefitted everyone but no one, it seemed, wanted to hear that. Universal health care meant just that: it was for all. But because the poor benefited and because the poor were perceived as not contributing to the nation's productivity, they were pilloried at the altar of political expediency. Universal health care was repealed and people who could no longer afford skyrocketing health insurance premiums began falling ill. People died and they were from all walks of life, not just the poor. Children and the elderly were first to die but they were soon followed by the young and healthy who, despite their vigor, could not resist the epidemics that swept the country.

"The exceptions were those with wealth and influence. Gradually, the middle class and the poor just gave up hope. They began staying

91

home on election days, assuming their vote didn't matter anyway. In a way, they were correct. That assured that those in control remained in power. Then when our Congress turned its attention to cutting programs like our own social security and our own Medicare and Medicaid programs, it was too late.

"The mentally ill went without treatment. Veterans physically or mentally wounded from our wars all over the world were left to wander the streets homeless and friendless—even as we congratulated ourselves for our support for our military, support that amounted to lip service and flag-waving but little else."

"So, did you wake up and vote the bastards out? Vasquez asked."

Johansson snorted his derision. "Oh, there were those of us who saw through all the double talk but the party just fell back on God and guns, God and guns. They wrapped themselves in a flag, raised a Bible in one hand and a gun in the other. Our people were just as hell-bent on gun ownership as yours. The gun crowd was supported by its national lobby which in turn propped up the politicians who were scared to death of crossing the lobby. We had mass killings and our elected officials were just as timid in addressing the problem. They offered their 'thoughts and prayers,' but said now was not the time to discuss gun control. We just experienced the trauma sooner than you. Remember what I told you: everything you went through, we did, too—only earlier."

"I heard you reference the Bible," I interrupted. "You had religion here, too?"

"Of course. Still do. We have our faith but we've learned not to rely on faith for everything. We have to help ourselves and not depend on God for everything. We take our own time and place for meditation and prayer, but we see to our own needs first. But we learned that lesson too late. We, and I mean we as a society, allowed the politicians to dictate our priority of electing those who professed their faith the loudest and those who shouted the loudest our rights to have arms. Never once did it occur to the gun rights advocates that our guns, pistols and hunting rifles were no more than pea shooters against the military weaponry that our police departments had been supplied with through surreptitious federal grants. Between the weapons superiority of the police and the military, we may as well have been armed with bows and arrows."

"I think Lars is getting ahead of himself," said Underwood, smiling.

"Not really," Lars said, pulling on his pipe. "Don't you think the protests were the cause of the war and not the result of it?"

"It's an interesting question," Underwood said. "But go on. Sorry I interrupted."

"Jim is correct," Johansson said. "It is an interesting question that still has never been answered to anyone's satisfaction because events become somewhat blurred from this point in our story. It's what you might call a chicken or egg question.

"At any rate, by the time the people awoke to the fact that they'd been used for the further enrichment of the already wealthy, it was too late. Yes, we had our guns but as I said, they were useless against the firepower possessed by the military and law enforcement whose loyalties had been bought by the politicians who were in the majority. The members of Congress who belonged to the minority party found their numbers shrinking with each election as the majority consolidated its power. And as more and more money was poured into their campaigns, more and more of their numbers were elected. And with each passing election, more and more abuses were heaped upon the people until one day the very party that had been such advocates of guns began confiscating those guns.

"That's when the riots started. People started ambushing law enforcement officials who came for their guns. But the protestors never had a chance. The police and military answered with overwhelming force, killing not only the protestors but family members who happened to be in the line of fire. It was carnage. Those opposed to Modell feared for their very lives and took to the remote mountains for refuge. They burned their homes, abandoned their jobs, their friends and families, taking only what they could pack into their vehicles. Modell's poll numbers, meanwhile, sank to an all-time low of twenty-two percent."

Johansson's face darkened with a special sadness as he recalled the hopelessness of those days.

"The only recourse for Modell to bring his approval ratings up was to launch a war against some perceived enemy," he said. "But by this time, he had become completely irrational, living in his own reality. His mental state by now was rooted in deep paranoia. So, to him, a conventional war was out of the question; it had to be a forceful preemptive strike, one for the history books, something truly spectacular.

93

"He launched a nuclear attack against four countries simultaneously, in two different parts of the world, thus assuring that this would be the final war of our existence."

Our host stopped and looked away, as if looking to the distant, lifeless mountains for the words to say. In reality, he was trying to compose himself as emotions welled up inside him, causing an inability to speak. When he looked back at the three of us, his face was streaked with tears. "You can't imagine the hell that was unleashed on us," he said, almost in a whisper. Meredith Sanders reached for his trembling hand and held it softly. The Terranum campsite, already quiet, suddenly seemed deathly silent as he continued.

"The attacks Modell launched were done so with no declaration of war," he said. "It was an arbitrary act carried out by a madman. The consequences of his miscalculation are impossible to describe. Can you imagine what retaliation from four different countries must have been like? Cable news never even made the announcements of our attacks before we had incoming missiles from every direction. The entire world was caught by surprise and we were as well. One moment, we were grilling hamburgers, playing with our kids or watching a ball game. The next, we were literally scrambling for our lives."

Johansson described the effects of temperatures so intense that entire cities at ground zero when the bombs struck were vaporized instantly. As the temperatures and radiation radiated outward, the air, heated to temperatures that defied measurement, was pushed like a piston, compressing and creating an expanding shock wave. At first, the shock wave was contained within the developing fireball but in a nano-second, the dense shock front completely obscured the fireball and continued to expand outward.

Most of the destruction caused by a nuclear detonation was the result of such blast effects. Virtually all buildings not disintegrated from the fireball were destroyed or heavily damaged by the shock wave which created winds that approached a thousand miles per second, compared to the eleven hundred-*feet*-per-second speed of sound. A category five hurricane produces winds of one hundred fifty-six miles per hour, making any comparison between the destructive capability of the two forces meaningless. Large trees were hurled about like so many toothpicks and boulders were scattered like pebbles, creating additional destructive forces.

The thermal radiation produced by an atomic explosion produces what is known as a "flash," which in turn results in horrific burns and eye injuries well beyond blast ranges. Flash blindness, caused by the initial excruciatingly bright flash of light generated by the detonation, results because the light energy is far more than the retina can tolerate and blindness can occur for nearly an hour. Far more serious is retina burn that results in permanent damage when the fireball is in the victim's field of vision.

"Thermal radiation can produce nearly half of the total energy released by an explosion," Johansson said. "Now multiply that by dozens of these explosions striking at once and you can only begin to grasp the magnitude of destruction that struck us in the matter of only a few minutes. To survive such devastation was a sentence more inhumane than for those who were killed in an instant. People suffered burns, blindness, hearing loss, broken bodies, open wounds. Our homes were destroyed, our food supplies wiped out. Family members disappeared without a trace. At least ninety percent of Terranum's population was wiped out instantly. The rest, those who remained, went from living in comfortable homes, holding decent jobs, and enjoying leisure time to shocked and wounded scavengers just trying to survive in a matter of seconds." His voice trailed off again as the three of us sat transfixed, trying to absorb the gravity of the horror Lars Johansson had just described in his brief but misery-laden narrative.

Just as suddenly, Johansson's voice grew hard and determined and his eyes, fixed on the three guests, were steely. His jaw thrust out as he pointed to each of us, individually, and began to speak again, his words chosen carefully and drawn out to emphasize the gravity of what he said.

"Ours is the fate that awaits your planet. Your course has been set and unless you intervene, catastrophe on a global scale is irreversible. You have a humanitarian duty to perform and you must not turn your back on that responsibility. To do so would be to sentence your planet to a slow death such as you see here."

18

Andrus Blount, who had run as a populist candidate positioned to fight high taxes, big banks, big oil, pharmaceutical companies and other special interests, quickly proved himself to be the ultimate plutocrat. He loaded his cabinet with Wall Street insiders even as he went about systematically reversing every progressive act of his predecessor. He managed to push through a bill he trumpeted as "tax reform," but which, in fact, amounted to a huge tax break for the wealthiest Americans. The bill simultaneously guaranteed the double whammy of an increase tax burden for the middle class and a trillion dollar increase in the national deficit.

Even though a large majority of Americans were not in favor of the tax bill as it was written, members of Blount's party in both houses of Congress held the majority and were either too timid or too greedy or too bought and paid for to resist the regressive nature of the bill and it passed by the thinnest of margins. The only ones who celebrated were Blount, his party, his rabid core supporters, and the very rich. The majority of Americans wrung their hands in despair and sought solace in the NFL playoffs, bowl games, and television reality shows.

When he couldn't get legislation passed, Blount appointees negated long-standing regulations of institutions like the Internet, cable television, and radio and TV station licensing by executive fiat. When something couldn't be overturned by legislation or agency regulation, Blount simply ruled by decree, employing the executive order to strike down regulations on the environment, banking, public land protection, and offshore drilling with the stroke of a pen.

Blount, the candidate who ran as the quintessential opponent of political correctness, became the principal Orwellian proponent of PC when, like *1984*'s Newspeak advocate Syme, he released a list of words forbidden to be spoken or written by federal employees. Words like "victim," "rights," "discrimination," "profiling," and even "sexual assault," "homeless," and "rape" were stricken from use by the Department of Justice. Likewise, "Entitlement," "fetus," "transgender," "gay rights," "pro-choice," and "disabled" were banned from usage by the Department of Health and Human Services. The Department of Environmental Protection, the Bureau of Indian Affairs, and the Department of Interior could no longer refer to "climate change," "science-based," "global warming," "sacred tribal land," or "Native-American."

The public outcry gave way to demonstrations which gave way to clubs and water cannons by police which gave way to riots which inevitably gave way to senseless deaths of American citizens attempting to exercise their First Amendment rights. The riots were quelled but not before cars and buildings were burned and gutted and blood ran in the streets. After it was all over and survivors tended to the injured and carried away the dead, Blount awarded medals of valor to the police "who kept America peaceful and protected American democracy."

Life went on but now military personnel patrolled the streets of the inner cities, which is what Blount sought all along. Minorities were pulled over and hauled in for no reason other than being caught outside after Blount's imposed curfew. Those who were not in the streets were huddled in their homes in fear of a knock on their doors. They could never be sure if it was someone who needed safe haven from the authorities or the police seeking some unfortunate miscreant.

Blount was spending more and more of his time at resort hotels in Florida, New Jersey, and other locales—all owned by him. The cost of the mini-vacations quickly ran to more than forty million dollars for travel and security in his first year in office alone. By staying at his own properties whenever he traveled to one golf resort or another, he personally profited from the block of rooms necessary for his entourage of aides and Secret Service personnel which was billed to the federal government. Wire services, electronic and print media accompanying the President also required accommodations—paid for by reporters' employers, of course, but nevertheless adding to the bottom line of Blount's hotels. If any reporter dared raise the issue of conflict of interest, he quickly found himself on the outside looking in—barred from all future travels and media briefings. Through it all, his iron fist rule tightened

In celebration of the new Gilded Age, underscored by the tax bill rammed through Congress, Blount boasted at a New Year's Eve party to his billionaire supporters who ponied up a quarter-million-dollar contribution to Blount's non-profit foundation for the privilege of attending, "You all just got a lot richer."

No one in the heartland of America heard. The bowl games were on and a national champion had to be crowned.

19

We could only stare silently at the tears staining the faces of Johansson, Underwood and Sanders. No one spoke for what seemed to be several minutes. Finally, Underwood picked up where Johansson left off.

"Modell launched the attacks with no provocation and with no prior warning. His generals were not consulted in advance. They had no time to prepare for the retaliation that was certain to come. It was madness, suicidal. We went about our affairs with no indication of what was to come and awoke the next morning to a holocaust you could never imagine." His voice broke, causing him to pause to compose himself before going on. His grave account of events only served to accent the stillness that enveloped the gathering as he continued.

"Billions of people and countless cities, towns and villages were wiped out all over the world in a matter of hours. There were few animals or vegetation left for food. Those in the heartlands of countries who weren't killed by the bombs soon starved or died from radiation. All who lived along existing coastlines were drowned by the rising seas created by the melting polar icecaps. Most of those who survived found themselves living along newly-created coastlines or on mountaintops which had been transformed into islands. Survivors were forced to learn to catch seafood to survive. We are among those survivors."

Meredith Sanders was next to speak.

"Your civilization has caught up with us," she said. "At most, you are only a few years behind us now. When you return, you will see the same catastrophic destruction of your planet as we have experienced here or you will perish in the inferno that will come—unless you act to change the course of your own destiny. You alone have the fate of bil-

101

lions of people in your hands."

Aboard the Sol Orbiter One, Wilhite, Patel, Bergmann, and Booth listened in stunned silence. It was interrupted only by Booth's quietly whispering, "Jesus Christ" when Sanders paused after her predictions to Whitten, Nguyen, and Vasquez. No one else spoke as they looked at one another. Wilhite witnessed the first signs of emotion from an otherwise stoic Bergmann. For a fleeting moment, he thought he saw tears well up in her eyes before she suddenly turned away. What once was concern for the safety of their compatriots on the ground gave way to a dread for the future of humanity in general and their families in particular, That dreaded thought settled like a heavy, wet blanket over the serenity of the Sol Orbiter One. Survival instincts suddenly trumped any feelings of nationalism, political ideology, social standing, patriotism, or individualism. Each person's thoughts were now focused on the very survival of mankind.

It was an unthinkable shift in paradigms.

20

Dr. Frederick Feinberg arose from the recliner in the den of his Hartford, Connecticut home. He had been trying to concentrate on a psychiatric journal but was finding it impossible to remain focused. He snapped the leash on his Basset Hound and together, they walked outside. The first TV ad would be running as a lead-in to the network newscasts in sixteen minutes and he was growing more apprehensive with each passing minute. He knew the ads would ignite a firestorm of criticism from the American Psychiatric Association. That criticism would pale in comparison to the vitriol that it would bring from Blount and his shrinking army of solid-core supporters. But of the two, his greatest concern was of the APA's reaction, which would be harshly critical of the breakaway Association of Patriotic Psychiatrists and its stated purpose—and the first ad had not even run yet. God only knew what the reaction would be once the ads began running.

He picked up the remote and clicked on the TV just two minutes before the scheduled airing. Fred, his Basset Hound lumbered into his lap as he returned to his recliner. Ninety seconds later, the thirty-second spot illuminated his flat screen Sony and an unflattering audio and video of Blount and incendiary images of his tweets exploded onto the screen. It was followed by a somber voiceover:

> "We've all seen him as he embarrassed America. We've heard him as he threatened the poor, the unfortunate, and the most vulnerable among us. We've read his tweeted messages of hate and venom directed at enemies and allies alike, even at members of his own party and cabinet. His words and his actions are not the words and actions

of a healthy individual. We have observed Andrus Blount for the past fifteen years as his mental stability has steadily deteriorated to the point that he represents a clear and present danger not only to the United States but to the entire world. Contact your senators and representatives and tell them it's time they stood up to this man before irreparable harm is done to humanity."

The message was followed by a brief disclaimer: *"Message paid for by Association of Patriotic Psychiatrists. A.P.P.: There's an APP for that."*

Dr. Feinberg wasn't prepared for what occurred next. The network newscast led with the story about APP's ad campaign, calling it "unprecedented." The complete ad was repeated as part of the news program, in effect giving APP a bonus in the form of a free airing before the widest possible audience. That was followed by a response from the White House spokespersons who called the ad reprehensible, irresponsible, unethical, and part of some cynical plot bent on destroying Blount and his presidency. More free publicity.

Within minutes, social media exploded with comments that swamped Facebook, Twitter and the oldest of them all, email. And then, along with the comments on APP's web page which were a general mix of condemnation and approval, came the biggest surprise of all. Contributions began pouring in via Paypal from all over the U.S. and from several countries. Most of the contributions were five and ten dollars, though some were for thousands of dollars. Over the next three days, APP, which had been financially strapped after paying for the network television ads, found itself with more than forty-seven million dollars in the bank—and donations were still coming in.

Feinberg and his fellow APP members were buoyed by this declaration of widespread support and their initial reaction was to think the response would have to awaken a slumbering Congress. They soon were disappointed as Blount's party rallied to his defense. APP was branded as a shill for the opposition, a purveyor of dirty tricks, and as disreputable outcasts from the better-known APA. It was a blistering attack but nothing compared to that of Blount himself, who wasted no time in going to Twitter to cast APP as "unamerican, communistic opportunists" out to destroy him. On through the night Blount continued sending out hundreds of tweets designed to rally his supporters and to undermine APP.

With such a vociferous core following, his strategy was an instant success. The APP Web and Facebook pages were bombarded with hate messages and threats of violence. Anyone who displayed a hint of support for APP or animosity toward Blount was subject to physical attack. And the more the ads ran in electronic and print media, the more vocal Blount became and the more his response incited violence across the American landscape. Civil discourse was out of the question as even minor disagreements quickly erupted in violent fights between Blount opponents and proponents. Blount, in a fit of unbridled rage, called on computer experts to hack into the APP Web page and on cue, several cyber attacks on the site occurred but the IT company APP had retained had included sufficient firewalls to prevent any real damage.

Some television stations, mostly those affiliated with networks on the right, refused to run the ads as did some newspapers aligned with Blount. Still, the APP soldiered on, determined to address the psychological problems permeating the Oval Office.

But every Blount tweet, every violent confrontation, every attack waged against the advertisement—predictably typical responses on his part—only served to give it more exposure and to underscore—and validate—its message.

Blount's push-back that he was, in fact, a genius who was far smarter than anyone else who ever occupied the White House. It was a silly, non-relevant response and it only served to give the APP free publicity it could not have otherwise purchased. People began to pay closer attention to the news stories about Dr. Feinberg and his upstart organization and to the ads that most TV and radio stations and newspapers were still running. That, of course, only caused Blount to become even more volatile in his outbursts and tweets which brought more attention to APP.

andrusblount@Verified *account*@POTUS.com *QUACK PSYCHITRISTS SICKER THAN THEIR PATIENTS. THEY NEED DOCTORS THEIRSELFS. SAD.*

andrusblount@Verified account@POTUS.com: *QUACK PISCHITRISTS MAY NEED LAWYERS MORE*

THAN DOCTORS. EXPECT MOTHER OF ALL LAWSUITS.

andrusblount@Verified *account*@POTUS.com: *PLAN-NING LAW REQUIRING MENTAL EXAMS OF QUACK PSYCHITRISTS. MY IQ HIGHER THAN ALL THEIRS COMBINED. LOSERS!*

Back and forth it went, like a runaway steel ball in a pinball machine gone amok. APP ads were met with protests and presidential tweets which served only to fan the flames of the escalating controversy. Violent outbursts by Blount supporters were met with more and more contributions to APP, which stepped up its ad campaign which prompted more protests and more tweets until any thoughts of accomplishment by either side were pushed to the background. Nightly network newscasts led with more frequent and more violent confrontations between pro- and anti-Blount groups and by reactions from Blount himself. The occasional plea from cooler heads to put an end to the rhetoric and for both sides to come together for the betterment of the country were routinely drowned out by the growing furor.

Other countries, friend and foe alike, looked on in horror. The more unstable America became, the more unstable the world stage became. Diplomatic negotiations were set aside since no one knew what the future held. Ill feelings between rival nations, previously held in check by delicate talks by emissaries, began to bubble to the surface as border skirmishes broke out. No one stepped up to ease the tensions. Blount responded to the growing tensions with still more tweets.

andrusblount@Verified *account*@POTUS.com: *Mid-east, Africa, Central America, Asia all have unstaple leadership. Probably will have to send troops to re-store order. Maybe even into Canada and Mexico.*

That tweet threw the media into a frenzy and the rest of the world reacted with immediate outrage. Blount, not surprisingly, seemed oblivious. The stock market plummeted overnight by more than three thousand points, adding economic panic to the political unrest. Beleaguered White

House Press Secretary Drew Mitchell, who had succeeded the fired Darla Rutledge, was sent out to do damage control. He tried to walk back the threats, asserting that Blount was "just kidding" about invading Canada and Mexico but reporters weren't buying his story.

"What kind of man would even say such a thing?" shouted a CNN reporter.

"Why would he even joke about something like that?" yelled a *Washington Post* political writer, a veteran of more than thirty years covering the White House. Mitchell wasn't given a chance to answer those questions before a *New York Times* reporter, Hansen Bridges, asked, "What has been the reaction from diplomatic circles?"

"The UN General Assembly is preparing a condemnation of the Blount's threats," came the voice of a reporter for Fox News. Fox had always supported Blount but now even it was repulsed by his behavior. "Has he gone completely off the rails?" said a reporter for the *St. Louis Post-Dispatch*. That question earned him an escort out of the briefing room over the explosion of protests from the press corps. Mitchell quickly ordered the entire room cleared, saying there would be no more briefings for the foreseeable future. Security promptly began wading into the throng of reporters, smashing cameras and grabbing reporters' notebooks. Mass hysteria ensued.

Blount promptly went on another tweet attack.

andrusblount@Verified   account@POTUS.com: *Lying reporters got a lesson for twisting news. Further justification for creation of my own news network. Only way to get truth out. No more WH briefings for lying reporters. I'm far smarter than all those sudo-writers.*

21

We were shown to our quarters where we would hopefully manage to rest although sleep now seemed out of the question. We had been given much over which to ponder and we were still trying to sort everything out in our minds. Tomorrow, we were scheduled take a quick tour of the area with Johansson and the others to see what the war had done to the land.

My room, which I assume was much like that of the other two—and for the rest of the settlement, for that matter—was part of a larger wood frame building. The wood was rough-hewn and not planed by a mill. The boards and joints fit haphazardly and the walls were not completely plumb. The building reminded me of the cabins I had seen in old movies about the poverty-stricken South and the pioneer West. There was no indoor plumbing, no heating other than a large central fireplace, and no air conditioning or even electricity, for that matter. My mattress and pillow were made of crude tacking stuffed with pine straw.

I removed my spacesuit after making certain my body cam was still functioning. The solar cells that powered it were supposed to last approximately sixteen hours after the last sunlight. Satisfied it was working, I collapsed onto the hard bed. I tossed and turned as the pine needles protruded through the cloth, pricking my skin. Still, I was grateful for the hospitality of the people here and for the chance to stretch out on the bed, makeshift as it was.

I lay staring into the darkness for what seemed like hours, thinking of what we had learned. It occurred to me that we had absorbed ourselves back home in speculation and research into possible life elsewhere in the universe. We had insisted on looking outward into the vast reaches of space. Of the billions of stars out there, we reasoned, the odds are there *must* be, there *has* to be, other planets with similar life-sustaining atmospheres. Perhaps there were even different atmospheric properties that supported intelligent life forms radically different than our own.

Once Mars was eliminated as a possible source of life, no further thought was given to our own solar system. Yet, here was Terranum, in our very own orbital path but one hundred eighty degrees from us, on the far side of the sun. They were far more advanced than we on Earth, even visiting us for two centuries and settling among undetected among us.

At least they *were* more advanced. All that had changed when they elected a crazed egomaniac as their leader. He promptly led the entire planet on the path to self-destruction, taking billions of people down with him. According to Johansson, every historical event that occurred on Earth had been preceded by identical events on Terranum. I found sleep difficult as these thoughts rambled through my brain. I was deeply disturbed, as I'm certain Nguyen and Vasquez were, by the prospects of a similar future back on Earth. If what Johansson had told us was true, that this now barren ball hurtling through space on the same orbital path and at the same speed as Earth but on the opposite side of the sun was the prototype for what lay in store for our own planet, then we must be doomed as well. How could it be that Earth was fated to suffer the same annihilation as this planet Terranum? It didn't seem possible. Yet, Johansson, Underwood and Sanders had taken us step by step through their own planet's experience of observing Earth for two hundred years.

They told dark, eerie tales of watching as Earth lurched through the same crises and hardships as they themselves had experienced, only earlier. The two planets were not entirely in sync as Terranum experienced some events a hundred years before Earth and others on much more recent time cycles. There was an unexplainable imbalance in the time sequence, perhaps brought about by some space-time differential as yet not discovered by scientists—one certainly not understood by mankind on either planet. But the one overriding fact that Johansson kept returning to was that Earth was gradually catching up with its sister planet in space and that it was destined to follow the same course of events, regardless of the timetable. And even though the precise time was unknown, the certainty was unmistakable. In due course, Earth itself would be thrown into its own self-inflicted Armageddon-like conflict from which it would emerge in ashes and ruin. It was the nuclear winter I'd read about. I found myself wishing as my mind slipped into restless slumber that I had read more about the subject.

I had no idea what time it was or how long I had slept but the sun was up and the compound was alive with activity. I found myself chuckling to myself at my absurd wish that I had packed regular clothing to wear—like some tourist on vacation—as I struggled into my suit, re-checked my recorder, and exited the building. "Well, good morning, Commander," came the voice of Johansson. Nguyen and Vasquez were already up and were standing off the side, talking. "You slept well?"

"Well enough to be the last one up," I answered, embarrassed to have overslept. I fell into step next to Johansson as I looked around at the local inhabitants going about their daily routine as if the three visitors were not even there. "What's on the agenda?" I asked. "We have to get away today, so we don't have more than a few hours."

"Actually, there is only one thing we'd like you to see," our host said. "We're living about halfway up what was once a medium altitude mountain. I'd like to take you to the top so you can see for yourself what sort of devastation a madman in a position of power can inflict on an entire world." In the space of only a couple of minutes, his voice had gone from upbeat and pleasant to the sadness and weariness of one whose hopes and dreams for an entire species had been forsaken.

We walked for more than an hour up a trail that wound through scrub brush that once struggled above the mountainous tree line but which now no longer even bothered. There was no longer living vegetation. Everything was reduced—much like the few million humans who now inhabited this planet—to merely scarred reminders of what once was and what eventually would cease altogether to exist. I was mesmerized at the matter-of-fact manner in which Johansson and the others had accepted their fate. I couldn't help wondering to myself if I could ever stare death in the face so calmly. In an earlier conversation we had attempted to encourage our hosts to not give up hope but Johansson quietly told him the effects of long-term radiation were already taking a toll on the remaining inhabitants. Two members of their small camp had died only days before the arrival of the Sol Orbiter One's crew.

We finally arrived at the mountain top that looked out over miles and miles of water interrupted by several solitary mountains that stood like lonely sentries with nothing left to protect. The other mountaintops appeared just as barren and lifeless as the one on which we now stood. Far across the stretch of water, I detected a faint wisp of smoke. Johansson anticipated my unasked question. "There are similar settlements on the other mountains. We're all friendly and don't raid or fight each other. That may be because there's nothing to raid. We visit occasionally, when there is a need. There's just not that much reason to. It's kind of ironic, I suppose, now that our civilization has been destroyed, we're more civilized as a people than ever before. Maybe it's because we all have a common goal of just trying to cope with the hand we've dealt ourselves." The sadness in his voice was palpable.

After a long silence, I finally spoke. "What caused the war?" he asked.

"A madman," came Johansson's response. He turned to face me. "You need to listen to what I'm about to tell you because you and your crew are the only ones who can prevent what has happened to Terranum from happening to Earth."

22

Blount seemed hell-bent on undermining his own presidency
before it even got off the ground. His business dealings with Russia had
extended back several decades and were reason enough to raise doubts
among national security personnel. He did nothing to assuage their fears
during his campaign after ascending to the presidency. His appointments
to key positions set off alarms throughout the State Department and the
National Security Administration, not to mention the media. His campaign manager, Steve Duncan, had worked with a leading Russian mafia
figure. Duncan himself had received millions of dollars in consulting
fees from Ukrainian politicians backed by the Kremlin.

Blount, who had billions tied up in energy production and brok-
ering, long had desired to tap into the oil- and natural gas-rich deposits
of Russia's Arctic Tundra. Still, it came as a surprise that he picked Robert Stillman, a man who had negotiated his own business deals with the
Russian oligarchs on behalf of his company, one of America's major oil
companies, as Secretary of State. Then again, maybe it shouldn't have
surprised anyone that the appointment smacked of insider deals created
to benefit Blount and his company.

When asked who his foreign policy adviser was, he abruptly gave
the name Adam Priest, a man who had spent a decade talking up Russia
at the expense of the United States, even giving speeches extolling the
virtues of Russian officials known to be KGB agents. Reporters agreed
among themselves that Blount only named Priest because he was pressed
by reporters and blurted the first name that came to mind. He was a man

with tenuous ties to the campaign until he was dispatched—by President-elect Blount—to Moscow to explore possible back channels for commercial real estate deals in Moscow.

His National Security Advisor was James Willis. His appointment was short-lived, however. Willis ran up his frequent flier miles on trips back and forth between New York and Moscow in secret negotiations with the Russians during the time between Blount's election and his inauguration. He received millions in contract payments from the Russian oligarchs who wished to cash in on the Blount brand. That those payments went unreported when Willis filled out the obligatory financial disclosure statements required of all cabinet nominees seemed of no consequence to Blount. But he was forced out in short order when the payments became public.

Blount even had a Russian partner in many of his real estate development ventures, Yuri Ostezenof, the son of a Russian mafia leader. Yuri worked diligently on behalf of Blount's election, promising Russian leaders that U.S. sanctions against Russia and several Russian banks would be lifted with his election. It was believed, but never proven, that the payments to Willis were somehow tied to Ostezenof's efforts to have the sanctions lifted. It was Yuri Ostezenof who landed Blount a fifty-million-dollar profit by purchasing a mold-infested Florida mansion for one hundred million dollars only to bulldoze the property before ever living in it. It was, investigators surmised, a classic Russian money-laundering scheme not unlike the sale of several of Blount's skyscraper apartments in New York City to Russian oligarchs for additional millions.

But what should have been the most controversial appointment was one that flew under the radar of senators at confirmation hearings. An American, Thurman Graves, had been head of an offshore bank in the British Virgin Islands that advertised online to offer "customized offshore protection plans tailored to your financial needs." It was a bank the CIA and the British MI6 had long before identified as a major money laundering conduit for illicit Russian organized crime financial operations. Graves had known KGB agents as his business partners at the bank. Yet, his nomination sailed through the Senate Commerce, Science and Transportation Committee in near robotic fashion with senators asking few questions. The full Senate then approved his appointment. Few in the Senate or the media appeared to pick up on the shady connections to Russian money laundering, KGB spies, and Russian organized crime.

Blount's attorney general was an elfin-like senator from South Carolina with a thick drawl who was transparent in his desire to take the country back to the fifties in terms of civil rights, women's rights, discrimination against gays, immigrants, and anyone else who did not fit his vision of the ideal conservative white protestant. Jews, Catholics, and just about any other religious belief that did not conform to those virtues were automatically relegated to second-class citizenship in his eyes. And he made no bones about his contempt for those with darker skins than his own bleached-white complexion. In all this, he had the blessings of his boss.

Other nominations to important positions raised eyebrows as well. His head of the Environmental Protection Agency harbored openly anti-environment sentiments and his Secretary of the Interior, charged with protecting federal land and national landmarks, instead advocated opening them up to oil exploration, over the protests of environmentalists and Native Americans alike.

He abruptly ordered nearly fifty U.S. attorneys to tender their resignations and then failed to move to fill the newly-created vacancies, throwing pending prosecutions of federal criminals into a state of turmoil and uncertainty. His choices for federal judgeships were nothing short of bizarre. The sole qualification of one nominee for the federal bench was that he was the husband of one of Blount's White House aides. Another, already the head of one federal agency was nominated for a judgeship but during his confirmation hearings, was unable to answer basic questions about law that a first-year law student would be expected to know. Realizing that he had been made a fool during his hearing, he mercifully withdrew from consideration before a confirmation vote could be taken. Still, it left the public and the media wondering what process he used to vet his nominees, if any.

To round out his inner circle, Blount appointed several family members as confidential advisers but neither Blount nor his immediate family ever divested themselves of their financial interests, leaving each of them in the unique but ethically-challenged position of being able to use the United States government to further their business interests. These included five-star hotels and restaurants, energy exploration and production companies, brokerage firms, and, in the case of his confidential assistant-daughter, a designer line of women's fashion.

Never before in the history of the republic had a president been so brazen. John F. Kennedy appointed his brother as attorney general which did raise a few eyebrows at the time. But at least Robert Kennedy took his job seriously and went after organized crime and corrupt labor unions with such zeal that some later speculated it may have led directly or indirectly to his brother's assassination. Blount's cadre, by contrast, exhibited an interest only in advancing their personal fortunes.

With the media becoming openly critical of many of his ill-advised moves, Blount retaliated in typical fashion. The news cycle naturally slows down on Fridays with reporters and the public alike gearing up for a relaxed weekend of golf, boating and other diversions to take their minds off the mind-numbing pressures of work and world events. Astute politicians learned that by announcing actions that might be unfavorable late on Fridays when reporters had gone for the day, they could usually dampen the effect of adverse publicity.

The end of the work week is generally known as "trash day" by elected officials. The least damaging time to get negative stories out of the way with as little public attention as possible is late Friday. If the story is picked up, so what? Saturday readership and cable news audiences are down and it's more difficult for reporters to get reactions from bureaucrats and elected officials. Blount probably learned that tactic quicker than most as public criticism of his administration gained momentum and intensity. He took the practice of the Friday News Dump to an entirely new level, taking unpopular actions and making negative announcements nearly every Friday during his first year in office.

If Blount learned the value of the Friday News Dump quickly, reporters learned just as quickly not to make firm plans for Friday evenings and editors began staying at work to perform makeovers for their front pages.

Some examples of Friday actions by Blount:
- Without consulting the legalities of his decree, he announced that he was instituting a ban on travel into the U.S. from several Islamic states. His order was promptly blocked by the courts as unconstitutional.
- His first nominee for federal office withdrew on a Friday after it was revealed the nominee had been convicted of a misdemean-

116

or for attacking a fellow spectator, a woman, at a professional basketball game.

- Knowing the law required the release of personal financial disclosures of nearly two hundred top aides, he delayed compliance until late on a Friday night, forcing reporters to scramble to examine the documents throughout the night.

- Blount announced the visitor logs for the White House would now be secret, a sharp change from his predecessor who had insisted that they be made public.

- When his surgeon general made public his opposition to e-cigarettes and his support for gun control, he was summarily dismissed—on a Friday. Blount's second nominee withdrew over comments he made about blacks, Hispanics and women, also on a Friday.

- All references to climate change and other scientific information pertaining to the climate were deleted from the Environmental Protection Agency's website.

- Blount's Attorney General, the race-baiting Geoff "the Elf" (he was five-foot-three) Bolin, a law-and-order fanatic of sorts, instructed the few federal prosecutors who remained to begin pushing the most severe penalties allowable under law, including mandatory minimum prison sentences, for nonviolent drug offenders. The owners of private prisons, who had made generous contributions to Blount's presidential campaign, were thus assured that they would continue to receive a steady stream of federal dollars for warehousing prisoners who they could in turn hire out to businesses in work release programs in which they would keep up to sixty percent of the prisoners' meager salaries.

- The husband of Blount's White House counselor withdrew from his nomination to head up the U.S. Justice Department's civil division as did a Wall Street banker who Blount had selected to head up the U.S. Treasury Department.

- The financial statement of Blount's National Security Adviser—and son-in-law—was quietly revised on a Friday to reflect that he had improperly neglected to disclose—a mere oversight, of course—assets worth nearly fifteen million dollars.

- Three of his appointees were fired on the same day. His director of the Office of Public Liaison and a special adviser left and a third, his chief of staff, learned of his firing by tweet— even as he waited in a Secret Service SUV on an airport tarmac for Blount to land. His vehicle quietly pulled away from the motorcade after the tweet was posted.

- As the nation's attention was diverted to the impending landfall of a category three hurricane on the Florida Gulf Coast, Nicolas Szheltzin was quietly removed from his seat on the National Security Council when it was learned Czechoslovakian police had an arrest warrant for Szheltzin on an outstanding weapons-smuggling charge. It was never learned what his precise duties were in the Blount White House or whether or not he held a security clearance.

As the Blount administration continued to spiral downward as the result of the multitude of self-inflicted wounds, the nation, including many of his one-time supporters, were already growing impatient and nervous about the direction he was taking the country. His hard-core supporters, on the other hand, couldn't have been happier. Oblivious to the warts on the frog, they could see only a prince who was the manifestation of their pent-up frustrations with the federal government.

Made up largely of lower-income, uneducated whites, this group resented the strides made by anyone who was not Caucasian. Mexicans were thieves and drug dealers, blacks were lazy and prone to drug-induced violence. Jews, Catholics, Asians and anyone else who did not fall into their demographic niche, were simply not to be trusted and Blount had promised to remedy all that. In their eyes, the ends justified the means and they were with him, no matter what the lying media might say about him.

And so it was that Blount had successfully cut a swath through the American social fabric, dividing it along philosophical, economic, and religious lines. Perhaps the least religious occupant in the White House's history, he was, nevertheless, the champion of the evangelical right. Now living with his third wife while continuing to have illicit affairs other women, he was nonetheless the darling of the family values bloc.

The nation had not been this divided since the Civil War nearly two centuries before.

23

$\mathbf{D}$r. Frederick Feinberg was growing more distraught with each passing day, with each new tweet or incomprehensible action by Blount. In his mind's eye, he saw in the Blount administration a metaphor for amoeba binary fission in which a single body separates into two new bodies. Like that amoeba, he could see a division developing between the administration of this lunatic and the nation's democratic principles. To Feinberg, Blount's idea of governing was to take the nation away from its roots by separating it from what had always made government work: the people of America. No longer was it a government of, by, or for the people. It had morphed into government by decree.

Intensifying his frustration was watching members of Congress fighting among themselves. In so doing, they were and failing to provide the checks and balances on which the government was based even as everything was falling apart. Nothing made sense anymore. The major news networks were pulling in opposite directions as well. One could watch one network report on some event in Washington and switch to another network and wonder if the reporters had been observing the same story unfold.

Spin. That was the operative word. Blount had his spin doctors distorting facts with their own version of the truth and friendly networks spread the word to the faithful. Unfriendly news networks and networks that purported to be neutral (as if that word could possibly hold any real meaning anymore) tried their best to sort the truth from the myth but they were finding their task increasingly difficult, if not impossible. Email rants shouted in all capital letters in efforts to be heard above the din.

Drew Mitchell was a buffoon and no one in the media, not even the friendly reporters, respected him. His disdain for the press was etched in his face each time he strode out for the daily press briefings which had been quietly reinstated by Blount. No one appeared to hate a job more than Mitchell. That's because the job of trying to interpret what his boss meant was impossible and the media didn't make his job any easier with its daily barrage of questions, challenges, and demands. Watching from his recliner at home, Dr. Feinberg felt that Mitchell might well be headed for a nervous breakdown. The psychiatrist detected a facial tic, virtually imperceptible at first but as the pressure of the job bore down on him, it was becoming more evident to a trained observer like Feinberg.

Likewise, reporters who covered the White House on a daily basis were reporting mounting tensions within Blount's tightknit inner circle. Blount was fighting with Congress, fighting with his own party, and fighting with a special prosecutor brought in to investigate possible links between Blount and Russian leaders. He was fighting with his cabinet and most recently, with his family. His wife, Renee Bienvenu, no longer appeared in public with him since rumors surfaced that he had paid off a porn star to conceal an extramarital affair that occurred less than a year into their marriage. When Blount traveled overseas, he was laughed at, jeered and booed. It was a jarring spectacle for the few career diplomatic employees who still remained at the State Department.

As the pressure mounted, however, Blount only became more obnoxious, more obstinate. He lashed out at those who criticized him. In his first year, he succeeded in alienating virtually everyone who mattered in Washington. But that only fueled the flames of passion for his core base, who grew bolder and nastier with each passing day. Taking their cue from POTUS, they felt they had carte blanche to attack minorities, women, gays, and anyone else who didn't fit in their exclusive demographic clique or who took issue with their political demagoguery.

Feinberg, between coordinating events for APP, keeping his practice up and running, and fretting over Blount's shenanigans, was losing sleep. He was losing hair, his appetite diminished, he began losing weight at an alarming rate and he had to force himself not to snap at his family over trivial matters. In short, his world, thanks to his preoccupation with what he considered to be a threat to all humanity, was closing in on him just as it was on Blount—for other reasons. He comforted himself in the knowledge that was all they had in common.

The social and economic upheaval wrought by radical policies imposed throughout the Blount administration was taking a toll elsewhere, as well. From the Atlantic to the Pacific coasts, from the Canadian to the Mexican borders, violence flared between factions with alarming frequency and intensity. Vehicles with perceived "wrong" political bumper stickers of all viewpoints were run off the road, occupants beaten and sometimes shot.

The sudden proliferation of Mexican or Israeli flags defiantly hoisted over homes and businesses was met with the equally insolent appearances of confederate flags and vulgar racist slogans splashed on bridges, overpasses and buildings. Those of the Islamic faith dared not show their countries' flags for fear for their lives. Mosques were burned to the ground and worshipers attacked and beaten. One home, constructed in the likeness of Monticello to honor Thomas Jefferson, was bombed when it was mistaken for a mosque.

And Washington's official reaction to all the carnage was a deafening silence.

As Feinberg watched the disintegration of justice, decency, and social order, he did so with growing apprehension, convinced that time was finally running out for America. Like Hitler, Blount was exploiting his base's fear and distrust of the unknown—Blacks, Hispanics, Islam—and that old bugaboo, big government. And like the days of Hitler and other ruthless dictators of history, it was fast becoming a physical liability to speak out lest helmeted riot police armed with water cannons—or worse—be called in to put down the so-called insurrection. There already had been enough cracked heads and imprisonments from sporadic outbursts to evidence that alarming development.

Even more disturbing than Blount's stated plans to launch his own television news network were several stories that broke on successive days. First, Blount advocated the nationalization of the nation's mobile broadband network. The proposal to give the federal government control of the 5G infrastructure was unprecedented. Though Blount called the proposal a safeguard against foreign cybersecurity and economic threats, red flags were immediately raised over the fear of government control of possible dissention through a shutdown of all social networking capabilities.

Before opposition could even be organized to that proposal, Blount supporters on Internet blogs and right-wing television news shows began making noises that were an echo of early twentieth century Germany in calling for persecution of those who were openly critical of Blount's administration. One TV news host called for a "cleansing" of the "unpatriotic in America" while a former FBI agent called for even more drastic measures—"the execution of traitors who do not stand up for America."

To drive home the point that the call for severe reprisals against dissenters was not merely rhetoric, the Blount administration leaked plans to conduct raids on the homes and offices of the mayors of New York, San Francisco, New Orleans, Boston, Chicago, and Seattle, among others, in a mass arrest of the top administrators of the so-called sanctuary cities. These were the cities whose mayors refused to cooperate with Immigration and Customs Enforcement (ICE) agents in its efforts to round up and deport illegal aliens. The Secretary of Homeland Security told the Senate Judiciary Committee that federal prosecutors, acting on his request, were exploring avenues available to arrest the uncooperative mayors for harboring immigrants.

And buried deep in his first State of the Union address to Congress was this statement: "Tonight, I am announcing my intention to issue an executive order authorizing every Cabinet secretary to reward good, patriotic workers and to remove any federal employee who is found to be undermining the best interests of the American people." Blount offered no criteria to determine who was "patriotic" or who might be "undermining" the best interest of American citizens. To Feinberg, it seemed a prelude to a wholesale purge of dissenters. It seemed a veiled threat to Blacks, Hispanics, gays, women or any other group Blount might target as "unpatriotic." The obscure statement which no one in the media picked up on smacked of the loyalty oaths imposed on Americans during the Red Scare of the nineteen forties and fifties.

The right-wing rhetoric was chilling and Feinberg and his contemporaries were taking it seriously. The silence from the media and from members of Congress—from both parties—gave them even greater cause for concern. They could perceive the opposition's voices being muted by the threats as Blount's Gestapo-like tactics were ramped up more with each passing day. Thus, they had no way of accurately gauging the passion with which the undercurrent of hatred for Blount was sweeping the country. But the festering antipathy among the disenfranchised and marginalized was a growing presence. And as is always the case in the births of revolutionary movements, once the rumbling began, it would metastasize like a cancerous growth.

Feinberg was acutely aware that APP, in its own way, was contributing to the unrest and the resulting threats to the citizenry, planting as it had the seeds of America's growing attention to Blount's probable mental incapacity. He could see the predicament that presented simply by watching CNN each night. He had hoped a submissive Congress, dominated by Blount's own party, would step in by at least rejecting his regressive ideas or at best by implementing impeachment proceedings.

Now, however, it was clear that even if a reluctant Congress awoke from its slumber and stood up to this tyrant, the consequences could well be calamitous as his lunatic-fringe base would almost certainly take matters into its own hands by attacking the media, minorities and political opponents. The alternative would be to allow Blount to continue his destructive and divisive policies. That, Feinberg was convinced, would lead inevitably to war, economic ruin, social disorder, and ultimately, the onset of lawlessness and civil collapse. With each passing day, the consequences for resistance became greater, instilling a fear in the hearts of Americans previously known only in Eastern Europe, Asia, and Third-World countries.

Although there was not a scenario he could imagine that would not lead to a national disaster of catastrophic proportions, he knew there was no turning back. The stakes were too high to risk failure.

24

Johansson looked tired. The long walk up the trail to the top of the mountain had taken its toll on his undernourished body. Finally, he sat down on a charred log, holding his hand-carved, six-foot-long walking stick vertically next to him as he did so. Taking a deep breath, he paused only briefly before continuing his lecture to the three of us.

"At the risk of repeating myself," he began, "I've told you about how we elected the monster Randall Modell and how he set events in motion that led to the sorry conditions you've found here on Terranum. And you've heard how all the events of your Earth tracked things that had already occurred on Terranum—the wars, the assassinations. The time schedules are difficult to predict because there seems to be no correlation. For example, our Civil War was nearly three hundred years ago and yours only about half that. But our two world wars were only a century before yours and our Vietnam was just seventy-five years ahead of Earth's. So, without scientific data, it would seem that your timetable may be catching up with us.

"So, at some point in the not too distant future, you will inevitably elect a madman comparable to our Modell…"

"I think we may have already done so," I interrupted. "His name is Andrus Blount."

Johansson's lips tightened and his jaws clinched as he stared off at another mountaintop across the still water. "I was afraid that might be the case," he finally said in a voice that was nearly inaudible. "If so, there is little time. You must leave immediately and return and when you do, you know what you have to do."

I didn't respond and far above us, in the Sol Orbiter One, Wilhite,

Patel, Bergmann, and Booth listened intently to my radio transmission of Johansson's advice. No one dared even take a breath as they waited for him to continue.

"You've seen what happened to Terranum when we chose a tyrant, a madman as our leader. He led our entire planet to extinction. We cannot survive for much longer here. There is no government, no shelter, no transportation, no food. Everything except the few fish we are able to catch are edible—and we're not entirely sure of that. Everything else is contaminated and will be for much longer than we could ever expect to live. We're a dying planet. Our demise is near."

For the first time since we met a day earlier, I could see the depth of Johansson's sadness. And for the first time, I understood that his grief was not for his own mortality but for the fate of his planet and its inhabitants—the plants, the animals, the birds, and the people. All were destroyed. What plants remained had struggled in vain to regenerate. With no bees or butterflies, there could be no pollination to perpetuate the species. No squirrels or rabbits scurried through the underbrush. No birds sang above them and even the few animals that did survive seemed as sad as Johansson, as if they understood their fate.

In the distance, a gray mass hid the sun and a chill enveloped the morning air. Johansson, struggling with each word now, continued in low, measured tones. "No one is going to believe you when you tell them about us. You can take something from Terranum with you as proof, but only those from our planet now living on your Earth will know and will understand. Find them, bring them into your plan…"

"What plan?" I forced myself to ask, even though I sensed the answer already.

"Must I really explain?" Johansson said, turning his one good eye to look at me. "You must make the decision to sacrifice yourselves for the very survival of Earth. Our people will do everything they can to assist you, even hide you from the authorities should you live that long.

"But you must, above all else, commit yourselves to the task of taking this man—you say his name is Blount?"

"Yes, Andrus Blount."

"You must, and I cannot stress this enough, you cannot be deterred from what must be done. *Take him out for the sake of Earth's survival!*"

126

Words stuck in my throat for the moment. I could only stare at our host. I couldn't bring myself to look at Nguyen and Vasquez who were exchanging terrified looks. At the same time, though, I think they understood the full gravity of what Johansson had just told us.

Aboard the Sol Orbiter One, silence continued as the four crew members looked at each other and then retreated into their own thoughts of family, friends, lovers. They had just been given what in all likelihood was a suicide mission, one that any true patriot, anyone who respected humanity, could not refuse. Finally, each went about his or her preparations for the return of the three explorers, knowing there would be many hours of discussions and planning, in the coming weeks before their rendezvous with a home planet they hoped they could save from annihilation. And there would be questions and doubts, as well.

None of them had signed up for this but no one gave even a fleeting thought to not answering this surreal call to duty.

25

Andrus Blount was in a foul mood. He was being bombarded by negative press, a couple of beauty queens were filing sexual harassment lawsuits against him, and the media had come across a two hundred thousand-dollar check he'd written one of them as hush money. His attorney general, Geoff Bolin, had knuckled under to pressure to recuse himself from an investigation of Blount's business and political alliances with Russia. His recusal had cleared the way for the appointment of a special prosecutor.

"What the hell does Bolin think he's doing? Blount thundered to no one in particular at his morning briefing. "Who is this goddamned Frederick Van Sykes? What do we know about him?"

"He's the special prosecutor," said National Security Adviser James Willis, unwisely answering what was a rhetorical question.

"Hell, I know he's the special prosecutor," Blount snapped, causing Willis to involuntarily shrink back in his chair. "But what do we know about him? Does he have any weaknesses?"

"He has a stellar reputation as a dogged prosecutor," said Foreign Policy Adviser Adam Priest, coming to the aid of Willis. "He is a plodder, very thorough, very meticulous, painstakingly so. He won't rush into anything."

"I don't give a damn about all that," Blount shot back. Priest knew he, like Willis, had failed to impress upon the President the gravity of the looming investigation, so he said nothing else. "I want to know what kind of person this Van Sykes guy is. Does he gamble? Is he a womanizer? Does he have a drinking problem? Problems at home? Does he need money?"

Everyone around the table—Willis, Priest, Commerce Secretary Thurman Graves, Press Secretary Drew Mitchell—exchanged worried glances. Each was harboring some variation of the same fear: *Surely, Blount wasn't suggesting blackmailing Van Sykes or worse, bribing him.*

"I want this chicken shit persecution stopped and I want it stopped now," Blount screamed, slamming his fist on the polished table. "If you can't do it, I'll have Bolin fire him…or I'll fire Bolin!"

"Sir, that would constitute obstruction of justice and you'd surely be impeached for that," said Willis. "That's what happened with Nixon."

"Andrew Jackson would've challenged him to a goddamn duel," Blount said, almost under his breath.

Then, he abruptly changed the subject, saying, "I haven't played golf in three days." Turning to Mitchell, he said, "Get everything ready to go to South Beach. I want to play."

And the General Accounting Office rang up another three million dollars in costs to transport Blount and his support staff to Florida for another weekend of golf.

26

"**B**efore we go any further, I want all of us to know there's no turning back so, if anyone wants out, tell me now."

I am career Army. A West Point graduate, I am proud that I've advanced on my career track as expected for someone who finished near the top of my class. My military career allowed me to escape the poverty of the Louisiana Delta. Now in my twenty-sixth year of active service, I am ingrained in the military tradition of following orders without question. But my one-and-a-half days on Terranum with the ravaged inhabitants has turned my orderly world upside down. It's no different for Nguyen and Vasquez, but they are subordinates; I am the commander of this mission that was supposed to be exploratory but which that abruptly turned into something else altogether.

Exploratory hardly described what I've seen and heard the past thirty-six hours. I looked at the smooth, flat stone the Terranum inhabitants had used to prepare their catch from the sea. It was the one item I'd brought with me to prove Sol Orbiter One had encountered an unknown planet and her crew had actually set foot on it. Johansson had inscribed the stone with the charcoal end of a burnt stick a simple message: *"Never shrink from doing what must be done."*

"Are there any questions about what we are to do we get home?" I asked, looking around the spacecraft at my silent but resolute crew.

Wilhite spoke first. "I think it's pretty clear what our duty is." Like myself, Wilhite was career military and had taken the same oath to obey all legal orders. Fully aware that what lay in store for us once we completed our solar orbit and set about activating our plan would be considered treason, no questions asked. He, like the others, knew none of us would likely survive. But when we considered the futures for our families, our country, and our planet, the choice became much easier to make than we could ever have thought. Then again, soldiers often rise to unexpected challenges in times of war and this was certainly a war for survival.

Bergmann, ever the pragmatist, known for her rational, unemotional manner, considered the logistics of the plan. "We can't rush into this without a plan of attack and an exit plan."

"Exit plan?" exclaimed Vasquez. "Man, they're gonna cut us down like weeds. We don't need no exit plans, we need insurance plans."

"There's always the chance of surviving this," Bergmann said in her calm, cogent manner. There may be Terranumites there to help us."

"Terranumites? Is that what they're called?" asked Booth.

"Who knows what they're called? That's as good a name as any. The point is, there may be help on Earth we don't know about yet. We need to take this slowly and methodically. Try to make contact, establish some sort of network. We can't just rush into the White House shooting up the place."

"Sarah's right," I said. "It won't hurt to take some time to see if we can make contact and formulate some sort of game plan."

The only one who had yet to speak was Dr. Hubballi Patel. Finally, she offered her thoughts. "We will need medicine and food in case we do survive and are forced into hiding. The…what did you call them, Sarah, Terranumites? The Terranumites might be able to assist us in establishing an operations center in the mountains unknown to the authorities, maybe in Canada. In the meantime, I can begin stockpiling medications, food and water. Colonel Whitten, can you obtain weapons?"

"That shouldn't be a problem," I said.

I looked at Wilhite, who said, "I think I can scare up a few toys.

132

We'll probably also need encrypted cell phones, electric generators, laptop computers, a couple of eighteen-wheelers and a helicopter. I can get the trucks and generators. Booth, Nguyen, can we count on you to procure the cell phones and laptops?"

"Certainly," Nguyen said.

"Absolutely. No problem," said Booth.

"Colonel Wilhite, can you get us a good deal on a late-model used helicopter?"

"Well, I won't be able to smuggle one out in a wheelbarrow, but I think I can pull that off," Wilhite said.

Bergmann interrupted the exchange. "There's something you all should know in the interest of full disclosure."

She paused as the others turned their attention to her. "I don't know if it matters at this point, but you should know that I voted for Blount. I felt he was supportive of Israel. That was my only takeaway from the election—his support of Israel. But now that I see that he's really a threat to the entire Middle East region, and the rest of the world, for that matter, I just want you to know I no longer have any loyalty to him."

Her crew mates glanced at each other for just a moment before Booth spoke up. "Well, hell, if we're going to bare our souls now, I guess I might as well admit I voted for the sonofabitch, too. But after what Colonel Whitten and the others saw and heard on Terranum, I don't see where we have a choice. Our first responsibility is to America and the survival of the planet. As far as I'm concerned, Blount's an obstacle, a threat, and must be eliminated."

Wilhite was the next to speak. "As one of two military officers with the honor to serve with you guys, I guess I may as well admit that I voted for him, too. He was—and is—a big supporter of the military. I guess he would have to be to talk the way he does about 'bloodying North Korea's nose' with a preemptive strike to teach 'em we mean business. But deep down, most military types actually want peace. We don't want war but we like a commander-in-chief who talks a tough game and Blount's done that. Having said that, I can't imagine any military leader carrying out an unlawful order to launch an unprovoked attack on a sovereign nation.

"But I heard the same thing all of you heard from Colonel Whitten's visit on Terranum. That guy Johansson had a wealth of knowledge

133

about us and he was dead-on with everything he said. The way I see it, we don't have any choice about what it is we have to do, but if anyone has any second thoughts or any doubts, now is the time to speak up. You will not be ostracized. We will listen to anything you have to say."

The only sound inside Sol Orbiter One was the low humming of the onboard computers and the air circulation system. No one offered any objections or alternative actions that we might pursue.

"All right, then," I said after several moments of silence. "I guess we're all in this together."

"We're with you all the way, Colonel," said Vasquez. "What's our plan?

"Sarah was very perceptive," I said. "We have to proceed with caution and be deliberate with each step. We have to try and make contact with any Terranumites living on Earth. They shouldn't be too hard to find. After all, if they know about our mission, they'll have to know we at least *saw* Terranum as we passed over. They'll probably reach out to us before we even begin looking for them.

"We will have to take them into our confidence. They haven't had any contact with Terranum for at least ten years now, so they'll know something is wrong back home. We can fill them in on what's happened there and alert them to what lies ahead on Earth. I can't imagine anything but full assistance in carrying out our operation.

"Also, Damon, did you happen to record what went on while we were on Terranum?"

"Every word," Colonel Wilhite answered.

"Great. We can use those recordings when we encounter the Terranumites to authenticate our story. But it's critical that we not let anyone from NASA or the military hear those recordings. We don't know who we can trust. Dr. Nguyen, Bergmann, can the two of you secure those recordings?"

"Yes," said Bergmann.

"Of course," Nguyen replied.

"Okay, great. Now, there's one last thing before we begin the detailed planning. I don't have to tell you this is an extremely dangerous assignment. Some or all of us may not survive and even if we do, we could be tried for murder and executed. But there are times when we must put the welfare of our fellow man above that of our own. That is particularly true in times of war. This is one of those times. We have to consider ourselves at war with tyranny. From this point forward, we have to think of President Blount in the same terms of despots like Hitler, Stalin, Pol Pot, Idi Amin, or Kim Jong Un. If one of us is killed in this war, it's up to the rest of us to carry on. Do each of you understand the gravity of this proposition?"

In unison, the six crew members under his command responded in the affirmative.

27

Things are seldom as they seem. Nowhere is that more accrate than in the nation's capital. Presidential candidates run on platforms of helping people, promoting economic growth, protecting the environment, providing health care, and ensuring national defense. And on governmental transparency. Once elected, priorities immediately change. The obligatory lip service is given to those same issues, of course, but the emphasis is shifted privately to fund-raising for the next election.

The only ones who can get an appointment with a representative or senator to discuss the economy are those in control of the hedge funds and banks on Wall Street—and they had better be carrying a campaign check with them when they arrive. Environmental concerns give way to appointments with lobbyists who want more oil drilling and fewer regulations restricting air, land, and water pollution. National defense is always uppermost with aircraft and munitions manufacturers laying out contributions and receiving fat defense contracts. And the issue of health care is monopolized by the giant pharmaceutical manufacturing companies, their lobbyists and generous contributions.

The voices of the American citizens, the ones on whose back the tax burdens are borne while the aforementioned enterprises continue to receive enormous tax breaks are lost in the din of Georgetown parties, back room deals, and political posturing between the two major parties. The concerns of the people are laid aside until the next election cycle, when they are pulled out of the closet, dusted off and trotted out for the TV campaign ads once again.

And the public keeps falling for the same old gambit, repeated every two years for the House of Representatives and one-third of the members of the U.S. Senate, whose six-year terms are staggered. For President, of course, it's every four years. Regardless of who is running for what, the same promises are made every campaign and if you are a challenger trying to crowd your way to the trough to chow down with the rest of the Beltway hogs, your promise is that you will go to Washington to fight for your constituents and to change the way things are done. The campaign promises, for the most part, are the same every election cycle. Only when there is a new political hot button such as illegal immigration or kneeling for the National Anthem is there any variation in the verbiage. But when all is said and done, it's still all just so much noise. If the challenger is fortunate enough to get himself elected, courage gives way to acquiescence and change surrenders to the status quo.

Each January, the president appears before a joint session of Congress, the U.S. Supreme Court justices, cabinet members, the Joint Chiefs of Staff and certain guests—inspirational individuals—from the heartland whom the president will recognize in his State of the Union Address. After the formalities, he will launch into an itemization of all the wonderful things his administration has accomplished and those which he hopes to push through the congress. It is a starry-eyed moment not unlike the various awards shows that populate the television networks in a given week: all glitter and little substance. More often than not, it is a dog and pony show to which the opposition party will respond with its own brand of partisan political rhetoric.

All in all, the pontificating done by both parties and by whomever happens to be the commander-in-chief does little to bring a disparate nation together. Rather than uniting behind a common objective, just the opposite has become the norm over the years. With more and more issues to divide the nation in terms of race, environment, social entitlements, wars both necessary and reckless, and an ever-widening gap between the haves and have-nots, there are few issues to bring America's citizens together, but many to drive a proverbial wedge between them.

And while the pundits and the amateur political philosophers shout at each other, trying to prove their side right by virtue of sheer volume, a smattering of quiet, objective citizens scattered across the landscape patiently observe the curious circus being played out in the nation's capital. The several state capitals get a local version of the same circus.

138

In a nation of three hundred twenty-five million people, those silent observers number less than five million. They don't constitute even a significant voting bloc because they are not concentrated in one state, but scattered among all fifty. Another thirty million, give or take a few hundred thousand, reside in all of the other civilized nations of the world. Some have been around for decades, their forebears dating back two centuries. Others have inhabited Earth for a shorter time, but none for fewer than ten years.

The Terranumites had been assimilating undetected into their environs for two centuries. Some came when the natives still rode horseback. For them, it was easy to enter into a society and to take up residence. There were no social security numbers, no radar to detect incoming aircraft. They quietly went about living as their neighbors lived while observing and sending reports back to Terranum. In only a few generations, it became evident that events playing out in their new home were the same as had occurred on Terranum years before, sometimes decades or centuries before—but always the same, at the same locations and involving people with the same names and titles. The same wars, the same economic depressions, the same elections, and the same political scandals.

The descendants of those early Terranumite pioneers lived on as citizens of their chosen countries, but they had their heritage passed down to them by their elders and they were strict in their resolve to not intermarry with residents of Earth in order to keep their bloodlines pure. As new arrivals entered from Terranum, they were met by their predecessors and briefed on their new homes.

As Earth's technology began to catch up, making their entries more difficult, it became necessary to develop counter-measures to avoid detection. Thus, was born the stealth craft to avoid radar, a technology passed on to America by Terranumites who had entered and risen to the highest ranks in the American military. Likewise, computer technology and fiber optics and laser development were the products of Terranumites. They were not in a hostile country, so there was no reason to conceal the technology. Issuing fake social security cards and other forms of identification was a simple matter as it was to integrate the new information into the nation's data banks.

The visitors—what else could you call them? —watched with

139

growing concern as the Blount phenomenon unfolded. They were at first amused at his cluelessness and then apprehensive over his incendiary campaign rhetoric, and finally, outright fear of his growing despotic pronouncements and his autocratic leanings. Through all that went on before, the Terranumites had clung tenaciously to their heritage through constant contact with their home planet. But there was concern and worry among them now. They had not heard anything from Terranum now for ten years. Something was wrong, they knew that much. But what? They had no way of learning until now.

They were all aware of the Sol Orbiter One mission, coming as it did two centuries after Terranum's own identical mission to Earth. There was almost no way the Sol Orbiter One crew would not at least observe Terranum, perhaps even visit. They would bring the announcement to the world of their discovery. Soon, they would receive word from Whitten, Wilhite, and the others about why they had heard nothing from their home planet in a decade.

28

Other than our shared newfound concerns for the future of mankind, the remainder of the voyage was uneventful, even routine. The crew was so well-versed with the duties to be carried out, each one went through the daily routine of checking temperatures, preparing logs, recording speeds, taking measurements, and calculating fuel usage (no minor concern, considering we had used thirty-six hours orbiting Terranum during our visit with Johansson) almost by rote.

As we approached our rendezvous with Earth, our apprehensions over our own fate intensified. My mind was occupied with many different possibilities and scenarios. Who would be the one to fire the fatal bullet and thus be sacrificed himself (or herself) in the name of treason or mental instability brought on by months of isolation in space? For that matter, how would the one who ultimately commits the deed maneuver into position to carry out the objective? And lurking in the backs of the minds was concern of a more personal nature. Would our families be cared for or ostracized in the emotional aftermath of a presidential assassination? I had no answers for any of those nagging questions.

Two months can take an eternity, or it can fly by in seconds. On the one hand, time crawled as we looked forward to returning home. On the other hand, there was never sufficient time to plan out such a deed as stalking an American president for elimination. In that respect, the two months to home was not nearly enough time.

Bergmann, ever the pragmatist, divided up the task ahead into compartmentalized segments. To her, patience was uppermost. To rush into something as portentous as termination with extreme prejudice, no matter who the intended victim was, required taking things slowly. We would have to maximize each opportunity and doing so quickly and decisively, no matter the immediate consequences. Her approach was more than calculated; it bordered on cold-blooded efficiency.

To Dr. Hubballi Patel, prime physical reflexes were crucial. Every move must be carried out with precision and for that, the executioner would have to be physically and mentally sharp, prepared to act in the split-second opportunity provided whenever, wherever, however. She decided that if the task ultimately fell to her, she would carry out the action and then immediately go limp, offering no resistance, in order to give herself the best chance of surviving the chaos that was certain to ensue. She was considerate enough to suggest that same tactic to the others.

Nguyen was of a similar mindset, steeling herself throughout the final two months of the trip to have the mental strength and discipline to show no emotion that would give away her intentions too early and then, when she was within striking distance, to do so quickly and then to turn her weapon upon herself before anyone else could claim the satisfaction of killing her.

Vasquez, the only one besides Whitten and Wilhite with any weapons training, preferred to attempt to carry out the assignment, should it fall on him to do so, with a high-powered, long-range rifle and to try and simply disappear, to fade into the background. He hoped that somehow, Blount could be lured to some place like Houston, with a heavy concentration of Hispanic population in order that he might more easily blend in. If he were lucky, he might even make it into Mexico where he would never be discovered. If none of those plans worked out and he could find no way out, oh well…

Booth, true to his electrical engineering background, tried to conjure up some exotic method of carrying out the assignment quietly, but in a way that would be just as lethal—and quick—as a bullet. His planning involved electronics, lasers and high frequencies. It was a method he knew might involve collateral damage, something he was willing to risk if it meant he could pull it off undetected, but only if the bystanders were the types who shared Blount's skewed values.

That left Wilhite and myself, the only two members of the crew who actually had combat experience, both having been deployed to Afghanistan and before that, to Iraq in Operation Enduring Freedom. We each thought along identical military-influenced lines. Whichever one of us the deed may fall to, it would be carried out as a military black-ops mission: quick in, make it a clean hit, quick out. If there was no way out, so be it: self-sacrifice for the greater good. Soldiers die in combat all the time. We were no different than any other combatant on a mission.

I kept thinking of a time when the citizens would just storm the castle with pitchforks. The logistics were certainly simpler then, almost amusing in their antiquity. Far more sophisticated tactics were required now. Never was any consideration given to going in as a mob or even a small group. That would be far too cumbersome and such a foolhardy attempt would be doomed from the start. This would have to be a one-person operation and if that one person failed, it would fall to the next to complete the mission against even tighter security. The one thing we all agreed on was the ideal spot for such an act: a golf course. Blount's passion was golf. He was unable to concentrate long enough on being president before he could no longer overcome the urge to head for the course at one of his luxury hotel properties in Florida, Texas, California, or New Jersey. When the desire to play a round struck, it didn't matter if it was the middle of the week, he had to play. All that was necessary was to make certain to be in the right place at the right time. It seemed simple enough in theory.

The big unknown was the Terranumites. Each of the seven crew members hoped in the back of our minds that some assistance might come from them, but it was something we knew we could not count on.

Reared faithfully in a Baptist church in rural Louisiana, I could not keep my thoughts from returning to the words of John 15:13 in the Bible: *Greater love hath no man than this, that a man lay down his life for his friends*. Or in this case, for mankind itself. I have to admit those words gave me some small comfort.

29

There were no more heroes' welcomes for returning astronauts, no parades, no invitations to the White House. Americans had become hardened to news of space travel since John Glenn became the first man to orbit the earth in 1962 or seven years later when Neil Armstrong first placed human footprints on the surface of the moon. All that now seemed a lifetime removed

The nation's attention returned to space travel briefly in the years following "One small step for man, one giant leap for mankind," but only because of tragedy. In 1967, a flash fire tore through the Apollo One command module during a launch rehearsal, killing astronauts Gus Grissom, Ed White and Roger Chaffee. The 1969 moon landing caused Americans to lay the catastrophe of two years earlier aside, at least temporarily. Then, in 1986, all seven crew members were lost in the disastrous Challenger explosion only seconds after liftoff. That was followed in 2003 by the breakup and disintegration of the space shuttle Columbia as it reentered Earth's atmosphere, again taking the lives of seven more crew members. The irony that we were a crew of seven wasn't lost on any of us.

But now, with the attention of a nervous nation fixated on the soap opera playing out in Washington, a tragicomedy that only served to further divide an already badly divided country, there was scant time to be given seven unknowns returning from a pleasure flight into space. And so it was that our mission was so overshadowed by the political turmoil in the West Wing that the story of our return from the precedent-setting exploratory mission was buried deep in the evening's network newscasts, well after the latest gossip from Washington and stories of mass shootings—stories separated by a flurry of pharmaceutical advertisements with legal disclaimers longer in length than the commercial messages—and just before the evening's cute kitten story.

Blount, for his part, was so oblivious to the potential importance of major new discoveries through space exploration, so restricted in his own narrow world view and his own self-absorption, that he never even extended the customary congratulatory telephone call to the crew. Following our debriefing by NASA, we quickly melted into the background, with only the most avid space junkie even knowing our names. An amazingly small percentage of Americans were even aware of the mission. Any one of the members of the Sol Orbiter One crew could have gone anywhere in the U.S. in the days immediately following our return and no one would recognize us. Not a single Sunday morning news show requested our appearance and no reporter sought an interview.

And to a person, that's the way we preferred it. Anonymity was our ally.

30

Jonathan Young was an exception. He was one of the few Americans who followed the story of Sol Orbiter One and its voyage two-thirds of the way around the sun. He savored every scrap of news about the mission. His father, Nathan, was a Terranumite who had been in Montana, living as a cattle rancher since he left Terranum as a young adventurer half-a-century earlier. His was one of the many hundreds of missions to Earth over a two-hundred-year period that mysteriously ended a decade ago. Nathan was twenty-three at the time. There was a nineteen-year-old beauty on the same voyage and she and Nathan were married a year after their arrival on Earth.

When Nathan returned to Terranum twenty years later to give an update on developments on Earth, twelve-year-old Jonathan had gone with him and he had been fascinated as he listened to his father brief the heads of state from several leading nations of Terranum on developments on Earth. He had taken note of how all had nodded as they scribbled notes as if they had anticipated everything his father told them—which, in fact, they had.

Now Jonathan was known as *Dr.* Young, a respected psychiatrist with a growing practice in Portland, Oregon. He also was a member of the Association of Patriotic Psychiatrists (APP). As perhaps the only member of APP who knew of Terranum's existence, one of the last things he learned from his father's home planet was of the election there of a tyrant. The tyrant had a cult following and his radical ideas appeared to be taking Terranum to the brink of economic and social ruin as the planet moved ever closer to cataclysmic social and economic disorder and nu-

147

clear war.

And then suddenly, ten years ago, everything came to an abrupt halt; there was no more communication from Terranum. Like the other Terranumites living on Earth, Jonathan and his father were at once curious and filled with the dread that something unimaginable had happened on their home planet.

It was with this concern for the unknown that Jonathan hoped to find some answers as he and Nathan prepared to travel to Houston to meet Colonel Travis Whitten and the other six members of his Sol Orbiter One crew.

31

After our encounter with Johansson and the Terranumites on their dying planet, there was little that could shock any of us. So, it came as no surprise when Jonathan Young reached out to me on Facebook. While I didn't know who or when it would be, I had been expecting that contact would be made at some point. It came only a few weeks after the return of Sol Orbiter One from our four-month mission. The message was brief and cryptic but, to me, self-explanatory:

Jonathan Young has a question about collecting terranums:

Knowing the importance of the message, I responded immediately, sending a private communication on Facebook's Messenger feature and then notified the others using the same method. Our initial meeting at a public library near my Houston home was set up in short order. Young was to look for me, a man wearing a Houston Astro baseball cap and jersey in the periodical section reading a *New York Times*. He was not to approach me directly but instead, was instructed to send me a text message as soon as he spotted me. At this early juncture, I couldn't be too careful and I was sure my contact felt the same.

I had been slowly turning the pages of *The Times* for about twenty minutes when I felt a familiar vibration from my cellphone which was on silent mode. The device's brief shudder told me know I had a text message. Casually taking my phone from my pocket, I read, "We're here." I replied, "Right-front parking lot, black GMC Yukon." I watched as Jonathan and his father casually exited the library before I arose, replaced *The Times* on the shelf and followed. I hit the remote on my keyring to unlock the vehicle's doors before I left the library. As I settled in behind the wheel, my guests were already seated in the Yukon. I glanced quickly around the parking lot. No one had seemed to have taken notice of our furtive rendezvous.

I started the Yukon and pulled out of the parking lot before anyone spoke. "How was your flight?" I finally asked.

"Not as eventful as yours, we're sure," came the reply from Nathan seated in the back seat. I glanced in the rearview mirror and our eyes met for the first time.

"We have a lot to talk about," I said. "Have you eaten?" It was 11:30 and I was starving.

"No," said Jonathan from the front passenger seat next to me.

Their answer didn't really matter because whether they were hungry or not, we were going to have lunch. I pulled into a nondescript steak and seafood restaurant in one of Houston's countless strip malls. "The food's excellent here and there're private rooms where we can talk," I said, killing the engine.

For the next three hours, they intermittently picked over their food and drinks as I devoured blackened salmon and we talked. There was much to say and both Jonathan and his father had many questions to ask about our visit to Terranum. "We were visited on a regular basis until ten years ago," Nathan said, "but then everything stopped. We haven't heard a word since then. We're afraid something went wrong."

"That's because there's nothing left there," I said. It was a blunt answer, perhaps too blunt and not nearly tactful enough but I knew no other way to broach the subject. "What was once a beautiful country with a highly-advanced civilization has been destroyed by nuclear war. There're only a few million people, basically scavengers, left on Terranum and all technology has been obliterated." I could see the sorrow on their faces as I related details of our visit with Lars Johansson and his tribesmen, leaving out nothing as I described the charred landscape, the sparse vegetation and the planet's half-starved population, mostly mutated from radiation—and dying slow, agonizing deaths.

Jonathan was impassive, even somewhat stoic, on hearing my horrific story. After all, he had been born and grew up on Earth, in America. He had no direct emotional ties to Terranum. Nathan, though, was another story altogether. The more I talked and the more descriptive I was about what we had witnessed, the more Nathan's face betrayed his pain. The picture I painted of his homeland was so unbearable at one point that he requested a break in order to compose himself. I tried to empathize with the emotional torture he was enduring but even after seeing the destruction up close, I found it impossible to experience his deeply personal feelings of despair.

When we resumed talking, I decided it was time for me to ask questions and for my two guests to provide some answers in order that a coherent picture of where we stood in terms of our common objectives so that some sort of cooperative endeavor to avert a repeat of that catastrophe could be pieced together. "America has some of the most advanced detection systems in existence to protect us against surprise attacks," I said. "How are you able to travel back and forth from Terranum without being detected?"

Nathan smiled as he explained. "What you consider as advanced would have been archaic on Terranum a century ago, maybe two centuries. You forget our scientific advancements were far ahead of yours until the war you've described." I had the gnawing sensation that Nathan was being somewhat smug, but at the same time, I knew the Terranumite was correct. "We had the stealth aircraft long before you," he continued. "We were able to slip in and out completely undetected."

Thank God they were friendlies, I thought to myself, trying hard not to imagine what they could have done if they'd been hostile. "Next question: how do you identify your fellow Terranumites? You're just like us, you've assimilated into our society for generations. There's nothing to distinguish you from us."

Nathan leaned back in his chair and cut his eyes to his son. Jonathan, who had been quietly sipping a beer, put his drink down and placed both his palms on the table as he turned to his father. "I guess he needs to know, Dad. If we're going to work together, we have to tell him."

Nathan nodded his agreement and then turned back to me. "It's so simple, it's really ridiculous," he said. "We hide in plain sight. We all drive only silver-colored vehicles. Trucks, sedans, SUVs, eighteen-wheelers… all silver. And each vehicle has an oval decal in the left-lower part of our rear windows. It's black with white capital letters that reads: TERRANUM."

I must have stared at him in disbelief for a full twenty seconds. "That's it?!" I exclaimed, laughing at the simplicity of it all. Suddenly, I knew why the word Terranum had eaten at his subconscious all this time.

He had seen that black oval decal before. But where? It seemed that every puzzle solved was supplanted by a new one.

"That's it," Nathan said. "Almost too easy, isn't it? But we wanted our method of identification to be as uncomplicated as possible, yet not obvious to others. And I'll bet you twenty dollars you can walk out into the parking lot right now and find a silver vehicle with that decal in the lower-left corner of the rear window."

I couldn't hide my astonishment. "Well, I have to say you're pretty well organized. I had no....no one had any idea, obviously."

"There's more," Jonathan said. "And that's our real reason for being here."

I sat without speaking for another hour, transfixed, as Jonathan told me about the Association of Patriotic Psychiatrists and its objectives to resist the tyrannical actions of Andrus Blount. As Jonathan spoke, I couldn't shake the uneasy feeling that the two men sitting across from me already knew about the new mission of the Sol Orbiter One crew. My initial fear was that I could not fully trust anyone. I wondered if a member of the crew had betrayed us. The thought that I was being set up flashed through my mind that was already in overload, having absorbed more information than it could process in a single setting. Still, I listened intently as Jonathan outlined APP's plan to bring down Blount on the evidence of his mental incapacity. I could feel my chest tighten as he spoke. My mouth was dry and my throat felt like sandpaper when I tried to swallow.

"We are prepared to do whatever it takes," Jonathan finally said as he locked eyes with me. I knew instinctively that this psychiatrist, this Terranumite, was perfectly willing to go beyond APP's stated objectives. And I knew without asking that when he said "we," he was not talking about his professional association. I gradually became convinced of his sincerity and began to relax—as much as a conspirator in a presidential assassination plot can relax. We exchanged phone numbers and set the time and place for our next meeting.

Finally, at a quarter of three, we left the restaurant and started walking toward my Yukon. On the way, we spotted seven silver vehicles in the parking lot. Two had black oval decals in the lower-left corner of their rear windows that read in white block letters: TERRANUM. No one said a word but I could feel a slight chill run up my spine.

32

As scandals broke all around him, Blount just dug his heels in deeper, attacking his detractors with vitriol not seen since the last hectic months of the Nixon administration. But even as he hastened the pace of his own assaults through his ultra-conservative news outlets, the mainstream news media reacted in kind. His administration was now engaged in a full-blown war being played out in the media and in the streets.

By now a special prosecutor had been appointed to investigate the real possibility that Blount was—and had been, even prior to his election, when he was still a private citizen—working with the Russians to ease sanctions in exchange for business opportunities in Russia for Blount's companies. In addition to finding clear evidence of that, which was by no means insignificant and a violation of the Logan Act, which makes it a crime for any unauthorized American citizen to negotiate with foreign governments having disputes with the U.S., The special prosecutor, Frederick Van Sykes, had stumbled upon a much more egregious crime in which Blount had likely participated with the Russians: money laundering.

As the walls closed in on Blount, his tweets became more and more disjointed and incoherent, evidence of a man with serious mental issues. Then a public relations disaster reminiscent of Nixon's 1973 "Saturday Night Massacre" occurred. On that fateful Saturday evening Nixon fired special prosecutor Archibald Cox. Attorney General Elliott Richardson and Deputy Attorney General William Ruckelshaus had immediately resigned in protest. Now events had come full circle as Blount sent out a tweet announcing he had fired Van Sykes. The big difference in this case was his attorney general, a southern lapdog he had plucked from an undistinguished career in the Senate, as expected of him, said and did nothing.

Both the news media and social media exploded. The nation was split along partisan lines, as might be expected, with most of the country reacting in outrage and Blount's solid thirty-five percent celebratory in mood. Both sides took to the streets and predictably, riots erupted across the American landscape. Even in the halls of Congress, members of the two parties, one supportive, the other opposed, blows were exchanged when debate turned to anger and anger to physical acts, underscoring the inability of a divided Congress to take definitive action to rein in the out-of-control chief executive.

Chaos was the order of the day as Blount, seemingly oblivious to the wound he had inflicted on the nation, boarded Air Force One for a weekend of golf at one of his resorts. He was, of course, anything but oblivious. Knowing the loyalty of his weak attorney general and the inability of Congress to agree on anything, he was looking beyond the immediate uproar his firing had caused. Once the dust settled, he was certain the Russian investigation would die a quiet death.

On the one hand, he projected an image that he was mentally incapable of being a world leader. On the other, just as he had done throughout his business career, he was secretive, manipulative, conniving, and shrewd.

In his first eighteen months in office, he dismantled a laundry list of regulations and programs designed to preserve the environment, protect Americans from practices designed to enrich lenders, provide health care for all, guarantee voter and minority rights, and to promote the arts. He pushed through a "tax reform" that gave massive—and permanent—tax breaks to the very rich while doling out crumbs, temporary at that, to the middle class who would be asked, as usual, to shoulder the burden for financing more and bigger wars by paying a disproportionate share of the costs.

And, ironically, with each move taken to increase the burden on the very ones who elected him, they applauded deliriously, proclaiming on radio talk shows that he had done "exactly what he said he'd do."

He then went on a presidential pardoning spree, freeing a curious cast of offenders, including politicians who had profiteered through insider trading while in office. Others had sold political appointments to the highest bidders and brutal law enforcement officers convicted of beatings and even killing prisoners were set free. His only explanation was that that each had been "railroaded" by an unfair system of justice. It was no coincidence in the eyes of many that it was the same system of justice that was now investigating Blount's own activities and associates.

But the most outrageous proposal, the one that added insult to injury, was Blount's decision to have the Pentagon hold a massive military parade in his honor that would make North Korea's leader look modest by comparison. Conservative estimates placed the cost of such an ostentatious display at ten million dollars while some said the cost could be as high as fifty million dollars. Most absurd of all was the fact that he drew his inspiration for the parade after watching a military parade in France, the nation that, the joke went, grew trees along the Champs Elysees in order that the German army might march in the shade. Sadly, the parade, as foolish as the idea seemed to nearly everyone concerned, was quite easily the most productive idea he'd had in his first eighteen months in office.

Dr. Frederick Feinberg watched this soap opera play out with growing apprehension and dread. It wasn't because he was feeling the economic pinch brought about by the cut in funding for mental health treatment—though he was. He could live with that. But he could not abide with the image of a man in a position to help but who was so disconnected with reality that he was completely devoid of the ability to emphasize or sympathize with the plight of the millions of Americans who desperately needed help. Nor could he find any patience with the man who would undo all the programs enacted to protect the environment, the economy, and the social fabric of the country.

For a man trained to keep his emotions in check while working to bring his patients out of their depression, their anxieties, their phobias, he found himself losing control of that one part of himself so essential in carrying out his professional duties to his patients. A psychiatrist in dire need of counseling himself is not a good thing. That much he knew.

That was why he finally arrived at a momentous decision. He would close his practice temporarily, referring his existing caseload to other therapists while he tried to sort things out in his own mind. That, of course, would mean stepping up his campaign within APP to bring about some kind of resolution to the Blount problem now afflicting the nation, indeed the world.

33

I sent out the message to the rest of Sol Orbiter One's crew via throwaway cell phone. Because there was a limited number of persons who had the phones, there was no need to identify myself so the message was short and cryptic: "Big party at my house Saturday, 6 p.m. Be there." It was a pre-arranged signal for the neo-cabal to meet. I wanted them to meet Jonathan and Nathan Young, who were staying in Houston for a couple of days. Every member of the crew lived in the Houston area, so it wasn't difficult to call such a meeting on short notice. My plan was to withhold, at least for the time-being, the information about the silver vehicles and decals as a stealthy means of identification for the Terran-umites and allow the Youngs the option of divulging information that sensitive.

The first to arrive was Wilhite, at 5:50 p.m. He was followed in short order by the remaining five. No one had informed family members of what we had seen and heard on the Sol Orbiter One mission, so each crew member came alone. School was out for summer vacation so Penny and the children were visiting her family in South Carolina, leaving me with the house to myself.

There was the usual socializing, complete with drinks and snacks, before everyone got down to business. I introduced Jonathan and Nathan without revealing their true identities, telling his crew members only that Jonathan was a psychiatrist who was a member of an organization that might be able to assist us.

To my surprise, Jonathan immediately went directly into why he and his father had traveled to Houston from Oregon and Montana. I hadn't expected him to lay his cards on the table so quickly. He spared no details of how the Terranumites had first visited Earth and how millions had quietly blended in with societies all over the planet as Asians, Blacks, Hispanics, Native Americans, Caucasian and other indigenous races.

It was a story that by now was familiar to all of us, thanks to our time with Johansson, but hearing it here, on planet Earth, presented an entirely different dynamic to the crew members, myself included. To all but one, that is. Suddenly, Vasquez stepped forward. "Would everyone come with me, please?" he said in a manner I found curious as he moved toward the door. Puzzled, we all followed, wondering why he would so suddenly—and rudely—interrupt such an important message from the Youngs.

With the other eight following closely behind, he strode straight to his vehicle parked in the drive, a Lexus LX SUV, silver in color. Walking to the rear of the vehicle on the driver's side, he pointed to his rear window and grinned like a Cheshire cat at the Youngs and the rest of us.

"You!" I bellowed as we stared at the black oval decal with the white block lettering that now screamed at us: TERRANUM. "You're a Terranumite? Jesus Christ!" The remaining five members of the Sol Orbiter One crew sucked in their breaths as one in a collective gasp. The Youngs burst out in laughter at the irony of it all. "Why didn't you say something?" asked an incredulous Wilhite.

"I couldn't," Vasquez shrugged. "And no, I'm not a Terranumite myself, but my father and mother are. I am merely a second generation descendent trying to preserve my heritage. My wife's parents are also Terranumites. You have no idea how I was about to burst during our visit to Terranum. I wanted so badly to tell you, but I could not. Only now do I feel free to do so."

Then Vasquez shifted and looked down briefly. "I know we are supposed to tell no one about what we found on our mission, but I had to tell someone. I just couldn't keep what I knew bottled up."

I, along with the others, stiffened, fearing our cover may have been compromised. "Who'd you tell, Rafael?" I never called subordinates by their first names unless I was upset with them.

"My parents. I thought because they are from Terranum, they should know."

I hesitated just long enough for Jonathan Young to speak. "I don't see that as a problem, Colonel. Terranumites are by necessity very secretive. We've been here for two centuries now and no one knows but the seven of you—make that six of you, since Rafael is one of us. Think about it, Colonel, who can his parents tell? Who would believe them?"

I looked around at the others. They nodded in agreement with Jonathan. "That's a good point, Commander," said Wilhite. "Who *could* they tell? If they did, they'd cart 'em off on the Disoriented Express to the Hotel Happiness."

I laughed along with everyone else at Wilhite's colloquialism in spite of the tension brought on by Vasquez's confession. Finally, I relented. "Okay, but guys, no one else is to ever know about Terranum, got it? This is serious stuff that could get us locked away for the rest of our lives and could scuttle our mission."

The irony of my talking about going to jail when we were plotting the execution of a world leader was not lost on us. Jail, after all, was the least of our problems if we were discovered. There have been nearly thirty attempts or serious threats on the lives of American presidents. Four were successful. Only a few of those threats or actual attempts were considered to be part of a plot involving more than a single person. I couldn't help recalling Johansson's cryptic words about Oswald's not being the lone Kennedy murderer. How would he have known that unless the Terranumites were involved in some way? Had he lied about their only observing and not interfering with events on Earth? Why hadn't I pushed harder for an explanation? The gravity of what we were contemplating suddenly hit me for the first time.

34

They happened almost back-to-back, occurring in such quick succession that Americans did not have sufficient time to recover from one traumatic event before they were accosted by the second mind-numbing tragedy. Both events would inflict further damage to an already badly wounded American psyche. The ensuing turmoil only served to drive the wedge dividing conservatives and liberals, whites and minorities, young and old, ever deeper. The groundswell of unrest reverberated through Congress and the White House and the aftershocks continued on to America's heartland.

It all began on a balmy Spring morning, a Monday, as the nation was emerging from winter and preparing for the annual opening day ritual of major league baseball. It had always been a time of renewed hope when grass reappears, birds sing and the air of America's ballparks are filled with the resonating sound of an ash bat making contact with a cowhide-covered spheroid bound by one hundred eight red stitches. It is a time when every diehard fan is convinced that this is the year his team will capture the elusive World Series ring.

That's the way it should have been on the quiet Southern college campus had it not been for a gathering of a hundred or so sullen—and armed—white nationalists. They had turned out to hear their hero, a frenzied, rumor-mongering talk show host who streamed his message of hate via the Internet to tens of thousands of avid racists and conspiracy theorists. They eagerly bought into his message that the commies, the blacks, the Islamics, and the Mexicans were coming for their guns and their women at any moment and they must remain vigilant against such imminent threats.

Lance Timmons, the self-anointed leader of this loose-knit band of militia wannabes who were going to save America from its enemies, was there to speak. The event was a rally of patriotic zealots who saw evil lurking in every corner of American society and conspiracy in every official government action. His inflammatory rhetoric was designed to whip his supporters into such a frenzy that they would empty their wallets to help finance his crusade for freedom and the American way and, if need be, empty their guns at anyone who tried to stop them.

And that's precisely how the trouble started.

A small group of protestors had gathered across the street from the building where Timmons was speaking. As his supporters exited following his address, they headed straight for the protestors, swinging clubs, pipes and knives, and waving guns with reckless abandon. The protestors tried to fight back with their protest signs but they were no match for the goons. Heads were split open, jaws and teeth were broken, some were stabbed and two were shot. Slow to respond riot police finally waded into the fray. Three people, from the group of protestors, were dead. Arrests would not be made until police reviewed video footage and even then, only one person was charged with a crime.

It took two full days for Blount to respond to the carnage. He was, after all, playing golf when it all went down, so why should he interrupt his downtime with matters that were of no concern to him. Finally, his handlers, such as they were, prevailed upon him to at least acknowledge the unfortunate deaths of the bystanders. Instead, as usual, he went off-script and began a rant about the actions of a few protesters attempting to disrupt a peaceful speech, causing events to spin out of control, which resulted in unnecessary deaths. In a circuitous fashion, what began as a condemnation of violence ended up as praise for the "peaceful" white nationalists.

The nation was aghast at his audacity. How could he defend Timmons and his crowd of thugs? It was an unconscionable, despicable thing to say. The network newscasts were filled with footage of the riots and the evidence was there for everyone to see. Except on the one network that shamelessly promoted and defended Blount in everything he said and did. No such footage appeared on that network and commentators were generally supportive of Timmons and Blount. Timmons and his supporters took that as validation of their actions and promptly went on the attack, citing his less than enthusiastic criticism of the violent attack by Timmons's followers as an endorsement for more overt acts of hatred. Online contributions to Timmons's Web page quadrupled overnight as sporadic attacks on blacks and Hispanics spiked across the landscape. Through it all, Blount and his supporters in Congress were eerily mute.

Before the nation could catch its breath from this latest outrage on the part of Blount and even as network news coverage continued its indignant coverage of the campus assault, tragedy struck again but this time the repercussions were far more widely felt.

The all-too-familiar sound of semi-automatic gunfire was heard again in a school. By the time police could respond, twenty-two high school students and three teachers at Franklin High School in Texas lay dead. Only the quick actions of a custodian kept the number from being higher. Jesus Rodriguez, a green card holder and a potential target of Blount for deportation, had worked at the school for six years. He was busily cleaning the boys' restrooms when Royce Brignac, a student, began his shooting rampage, spraying the hallways with an AR-15.

As the shooter made his way down the school's corridor, firing indiscriminately as he advanced, Rodriguez could hear the screams of Brignac's terrified victims mixed in with the sounds of deadly gunfire and the ricocheting bullets. The only weapon at his disposal was a mop but it was a commercial mop with a thick wooden handle. He laid it on the floor and, standing with one foot on the base, gave the other end a quick pull upward, snapping the handle in too. Holding what now amounted to a club about three-and-a-half feet in length and with no regard for his own safety, he crept to the door of the restroom and spotted Brignac about forty feet away, with his back to Rodriguez. His heart pounding, Rodriguez covered the distance in a burst of speed, swinging as he did so with every ounce of strength his body possessed.

His aim was dead-on in every literal sense of the term. The crack of the mop handled echoed through the hallway as it shattered across the base of Brignac's skull. The assailant crumpled in a heap, the AR-15 sliding away from him, down the hallway. Rodriguez could see the blood oozing from Brignac's head but he began pummeling and cursing the unconscious killer anyway as several male students, aware the shooter had been neutralized, piled out of classrooms to lend assistance that by now was unnecessary.

The first police officers to arrive, mistakenly thinking Rodriguez was the shooter promptly grabbed him and pinned him to the ground in the confusion. Even as guns were held to his head, students began screaming that Rodriquez was not the shooter. One officer managed to deliver a brutal kick to Rodriguez's ribs before the students' protests finally got through. Still, the officers were reluctant to let him up from the floor. It was Rusty Weber who finally got through to them. "You bastards, leave him alone! He saved us. *There's* your shooter!"

The officers looked over at Brignac and one of them bent down to take a pulse. "Dead," he said, looking up. Then, to the students, "How'd he die?"

"Rodriguez took him down," Weber said.

"How'd you do that" the officer asked Rodriguez.

"With a mop."

"You took on an AR-15 with a mop?"

"I had to do something. People were dying."

Authorities began clearing the building room by room and then went about with the body count of yet another school shooting in America.

That evening, millions watched the evening news to learn more children had died as the result of easy access to assault weapons. At the same time, they heard the usual utterances of "thoughts and prayers" for the victims and "now is not the time" to discuss gun control, a theme that had become almost a cliché in the American vernacular. They had become time-worn phrases that no longer held any meaning.

At the same time, America had a new authentic hero. His name was Jesus Rodriguez and he represented the hundreds of thousands of Hispanics Blount wanted deported.

And America had a new spokesperson for gun control. Or more correctly, spokespersons. the entire student body of Franklin High School who would take on Congress, President Blount and an even more powerful foe, The American Rifle and Munitions Society (ARMS) lobby.

164

35

It might have been just another school shooting, an event that prompted somber-faced politicians to proclaim that their "thoughts and prayers" were with the victims' families but "this was just not the time to discuss limiting access to assault weapons." The phrase thoughts and prayers quickly became known by the acronym TAPs by an outraged public more and more fed up with congressional inaction. But TAPs represented the extent to which members of Congress were willing to stick their political necks out. Their desire to continue receiving generous campaign contributions from the American Rifle and Munitions Society trumped any desire to effect meaningful gun control legislation. Campaign contributions reigned over moral obligations and made the ARMS one of the most powerful lobbyists inside the Beltway.

But it wasn't just another shooting—for several reasons. One, there had been too many already and the nation's patience with Congress was already stretched thin on several issues, but on gun control in particular. Second, this shooting wasn't at an elementary school where the surviving children had no public voice; it was at an upscale high school where the majority of the student body consisted of over-achievers who were intelligent, articulate, and irreverent enough to speak out. And speak out they did, challenging the mindset of Congress that had been far too long devoted to the rights of hunters to keep their weapons—as if mass shooters could in some way be considered as hunters.

The students had barely begun their campaign for the passage of saner gun laws when the American Firearms Coalition launched its counter-attack, branding the students as imposters, as professional crisis exploiters. Some, members of the lunatic fringe, even claimed the shootings did not occur, that the story was a hoax designed to incite Americans to support the confiscation of firearms and the abolition of the Second Amendment. Others, taking what they thought was a more subdued approach, pointed to the protestors' youthful inexperience in the political arena.

The strategy could not have been any more ill-advised. Americans were not prepared to see the victims pilloried so soon after the shooting spree. The backlash was instant and it was harsh. In the midst of the pitched rhetoric, two students emerged as leaders of the Franklin students. They would become the symbolic face of the gun control movement that began sweeping the land. Lacy Hernandez and Ray Trout were mature for their eighteen years. Both were honor students and both possessed the personalities necessary for militancy. The metaphorically locked arms with the rest of the student body and stood up to the American Firearms Coalition and the politicians it propped up with its campaign contributions. Hernandez and Trout, with the assistance of a willing media, quickly trotted out a list of the members of Congress who were the biggest recipients of coalition campaign funds. The faces of the senators and representatives were plastered all over the Internet, on posters, and in the print and electronic media for all to see.

Suddenly, the students, initially labeled as immature, irresponsible, and naïve, emerged as the adults in the room as the national debate moved to the Sunday morning network political talk shows and the evening newscasts. Blount's feeble attempt to defuse the situation with a televised meeting with relatives of shooting victims drew instant ridicule when a TV camera close-up of his handwritten crib notes revealed the stark truth. The notes contained cryptic talking points for Blount prepared by his handlers. The cheat sheet clearly showed for viewers to see words like "empathy," "painful," "sympathy," "shock," and "outrage." They were words no normal person would need to jot down in advance; they were the words that would naturally come from any ordinary individual without the need for prompting.

But Blount was neither normal nor ordinary and the nation was given a firsthand look at the superficiality of his makeup, his phoniness, and his insincerity. And it did not play well to a national audience still reeling from the shock of another assault on school children by a mentally deranged person with easy access to an assault weapon. The presi-

166

dent's approval ratings, already low, plummeted even further overnight.

But rather than appearing contrite over his blundering faux pas, Blount did what he always did. He went on the offense, conjuring up more tweets about the necessity to launch a war with perceived enemies: "Atrocities in Syria, North Korea. Bad people must be eliminated. U.S. has firepower to do what must be done. My button is bigger than their button."

The Pentagon, as well as the White House staff, was caught completely off guard. No one knew how to react to his inflammatory tweet, least of all diplomats whose job it was to keep the peace through tactful negotiations.

The one group that was not surprised, however, was Dr. Frederick Feinberg and his Association of Patriotic Psychiatrists. Feinberg watched the entire scene unfold on network television and immediately sent out a call to action: "Urgent: Situation deteriorating. Emergency board meeting necessary soonest. Please give your availability ASAP so meeting may be scheduled."

36

Andrus Blount was in a good mood for a change. He had pushed through a tax bill while convincing his core supporters, the blue-collar Americans, that the tax reform bill was to help relieve their tax burden. It in fact did little to benefit working Americans but was a major benefit for the super-rich. He had reduced health care benefits drastically. Bankers were again free to proceed with their reckless investments of customers' funds.

He had succeeded in alienating virtually all of America's allies while cozying up to perceived enemies—Russia, North Korea, and China. What had begun as major import sanctions on China's products turned into economic aid for a major Chinese computer chip manufacturer when several of Blount's companies were quietly given China trademarks.

He was contemplating costly tariffs on products from the rest of the world, a tactic he was confident would restore America as the world's leading producer of good instead of her current status as a consumer—a lending nation instead of a borrower. But as was his custom, he had never looked beyond whatever short-term gains might be realized, nor had he weighed them against the long-term costs of a protracted trade war.

All that wasn't to say his administration wasn't being touched by an endless parade of official scandals. You could start with just about any agency or department—DHH, EPA, FBI, Interior, State, FCC—and you would find a major scandal, sometimes more than one, occurring simultaneously.

And of course, there was always Frederick Van Sykes, the damned special prosecutor, who wouldn't give Blount a moment's peace. Nor would the media hounds.

But today was different. He had opted for a weekend of golf at his resort hotel and golf club at South Beach and the weather was so beautiful that he abruptly cancelled all his appointments for Monday to stay over another day.

That's what he was doing when he heard about the shootings at Franklin High School in Texas. But what the hell? That was in Texas, five states away and by God, they loved guns in Texas. What could he do in Florida? So, he finished his round.

37

I couldn't believe Blount was actually threatening to go to war. Things were spinning out of control quickly. I called an emergency meeting of our junta. Phobe and the kids were back home from visiting her family, so I set the assembly for 7:00 p.m. in a conference room of a local hotel near George Bush Intercontinental Airport. I instructed Vasquez to invite several of his fellow Terranumites. "This meeting will be to set in motion our final objective for the annual flower show," I explained in our predetermined code that signaled to everyone that we were now past the point of no return and in the final phase of our plan to take out Blount once and for all. In spite of my training as a professional soldier, I couldn't help noticing that my hand trembled as I typed my text message. I received six affirmative responses within thirty seconds of sending the message. Everyone was on board. We were officially at war, albeit undeclared, with the government of the United States of America—or at least with the person positioned as leader of that government.

It would be futile to attempt to describe the range of gut-wrenching emotions I experienced as I sent out the call. After hitting *send* on my cell phone, I went straight to the bathroom and threw up. I suspected my crew members were doing the same.

38

Jonathan Young in Oregon and his father, Nathan, in Montana watched the evening news and learned of Blount's reckless tweets at the same time. Each had a list that contained a name and phone numbers. The person whose name was on each subsequent list also had a name and number to call. Simultaneously, texts went out to an inner circle of fellow Terranumites, a dozen trained marksmen who had served in the U.S. military. Not to be confused with overweight, loud-mouthed self-proclaimed citizen militia types, these veterans specially trained Navy Seal and Special Forces personnel who, though no longer active military, had nevertheless continued to train quietly and efficiently, away from the public eye.

They were led by Bob Hastings, a third-generation Terranumite who had served three tours in the Mideast, rising to the rank of major before retiring to the remote hills of southern Idaho where he continued to train the handful of dedicated men under his command, each of whom was trained to kill quickly, quietly, and efficiently. Each, in fact, *had* killed in combat. They had fervently hoped their services would never be called upon. But now they stood ready, a lethal force ready to act when needed. Because they were a small group, they were mobile, quick in and quick out, capable of inflicting heavy damage on a much larger force and then able to vanish without so much as a trace that they ever existed.

The entire contingent, fully equipped and battle-ready, was assembled within four hours. Hastings split them into three units of four in order to lessen any chance of discovery or capture and to increase the odds of success in case one unit failed to reach its destination.

Teams or individuals were dispatched to Florida, Texas and New

173

Jersey—states where Blount owned resort hotels and golf courses, or where Blount was scheduled to speak to supporters. He also owned a golf resort in California, a state he loathed. He had never visited that club during his brief presidency so no one was sent there from APP or the Terranumite elite forces. One member of Whitten's team was sent there, just in case.

39

I knew the APP existed as a group only through seeing their ads on television and in newspapers. I watched as they ramped up their advertisements each time Blount did something outrageous so I was a little curious when they didn't react to his threats of war with a new barrage of ads. I also was aware of the separate activities being planned by the Youngs through our constant exchange of cryptic communications. But I didn't know about their crack team of military veterans because they played their cards so close to their vests, choosing not to share too much information out of concern for leaks. I assumed the extent of their activity was through cooperative endeavors with our group which were being coordinated by Vasquez. They, in turn, knew little of our plans for the same concerns for security and secrecy. APP, on the other hand, was sharing information with no one. Our group and the Terranumites operated independently of each other and neither group knew any details of the plans or operations of the other.

It was a formula for disaster or guaranteed success but no one could predict either outcome even if they had access to all the plans being executed.

Just to be certain all our bases were covered, I sent Nguyen Huy to California even though there was no real reason to believe Blount would show up there.

All any of us could do now was sit and wait for Blount to choose one of his resorts at which to play golf. No one had any idea which course he would choose—or when. And we had only the vaguest idea of how to get close enough with our CheyTac Intervention sniper rifles. At thirty-one pounds, the weapon is a little heavy for optimum mobility but its capability of precision accuracy at more than two thousand meters [almost a one and one-half miles] offsets any weight disadvantage.

I only *thought* space travel around the sun was a tension-packed adventure. That was nothing compared to the kaleidoscope of thoughts of the participants as we prepared for what would likely be described by the history books as a cold-blooded act of treason.

It's hard to explain, but time can slow to a snail's pace and become a blur of activity at the same time. On the one hand, a highlight film of your life plays out in your mind one agonizing day at a time while on the other, events move at a dizzying pace and make it impossible to keep pace. I was chewing antacid tablets like candy in an attempt to quell the burning that was eating up my gut. Having never been deployed to the Mideast, I can only imagine my anxiety level was approaching that experienced by soldiers clad in bulky protective uniforms in the unbearable heat of the desert while trying to avoid snipers and IEDs.

It was an unfair comparison; in one scenario, men and women were trying to survive to get back home to loved ones while in the other, there was the full knowledge that whoever was on the team that successfully took out the President of the United States would never see the dawning of another day.

In the interest of security and of protecting each team member, sealed envelopes were passed out with instructions not to open them until each member was alone. The envelopes contained destination assignments. Each member was to make his or her own travel and lodging arrangements. No other team member, other than the person each was partnered with, if they were partnered, was to ever know who was sent where. I thought that was the best way to avoid leaks as well as a way to spare undue pressure on other members of the team to give up information if we were ever found out. If we didn't know anything, we couldn't give anyone up.

With the long-range sniper rifles, we were trying to give ourselves the best chance of escaping without detection. At the same time, a crime of this magnitude would result in the most intensive manhunt since the Kennedy assassination and only a series of extremely fortuitous strokes of luck would allow us to come out of this alive. I kept thinking about Phoebe and the kids and my eighty-three-year-old dad who still lived in northeast Louisiana. A life devoted to my country and my family had come down to this moment. We tried to tell ourselves we were prepared to die for the cause of humanity but deep down, no one wants to die and certainly no one wants to bring disgrace on himself and his family in the process. I'm certain most of us were praying in our own private way.

I know I was, as Daryl Booth and I headed for South Beach, Florida, that strip of prime real estate between Biscayne Bay and the Atlantic Ocean. We were on separate flights, of course. The rumor, unconfirmed by the White House, was that Blount might make a surprise appearance before the membership of the American Rifle and Munitions Society convention there and more than ten thousand ARMS members were expected to be on hand to hear him if he did. But that was speculation, for Blount seldom planned more than a few hours ahead, so it was anyone's guess if he would be there or at one of his resorts playing golf.

I couldn't help but wonder if Booth was experiencing the same range of emotions as I was. He had never been in the military but I never had any reason to question his bravery and I certainly didn't now. He never signed up for something like this but once he saw what had occurred on Terranum, his commitment was total. And while I had ever confidence in his dedication, his inexperience as a trained killer gave me pause for concern. Would he freeze up in the moment of truth? Professional soldiers had done so in the midst of battle, so it wasn't unreasonable to harbor doubts. And those doubts caused me to feel guilty as hell.

Sarah Bergmann's orders directed her to San Antonio. She drove there from Houston. Dr. Hubballi Patel quietly caught a flight for Atlantic City, New Jersey. Colonel Damon Wilhite remained behind in Houston to serve as point man and Vasquez was with the Terranumite recruits assigning teams of two to the same locations. One extra team was sent to Washington—in the unlikely event that Blount decided to remain at the White House for the weekend.

Bergmann likewise had no military experience but for some reason buried deep within my psyche, I knew her ingrained pragmatism would see her through whatever crisis she encountered—including a diabolical plot to assassinate the leader of the free world. I wished I could have the same confidence in Dr. Patel, a man trained his entire professional life to save lives, not snuff them out. On the other hand, I had no choice but to depend on him to come through for the greater cause of the survival of humanity.

I had no qualms whatsoever about Wilhite and Vasquez. Though Wilhite, like me, had never been deployed, his son had—twice. And despite his lack of actual battle experience, he was career Air Force and had undergone all the prerequisite training for warfare as a graduate of the Air Force Academy. His steady composure as a top NASA pilot was more than sufficient testimony to his ability to function under extreme pressure. My biggest concern for Wilhite was the emotional toll on him. His son was an Air Force pilot, twice deployed to the Mideast. Should Damon ultimately be on the team that carried out the assassination or if he was in any manner identified with the conspiracy, how would it affect the son's career? Or perhaps more importantly, his life? That question must be tormenting him more than the rest of us could ever imagine. Vasquez, as a closet Terranumite, was every bit as dependable as the most battle-veteran GI. His rising from his El Paso barrio background only further strengthened his resolve to do whatever was necessary to not just survive, but to excel under the most adverse circumstances.

America had grown soft in the years following World War II. We had, become comfortable in our cookie-cutter suburban homes on our wide, paved streets with nice concrete sidewalks and subdivision covenants. In our relatively secure bubbles of existence we had, seriously underestimated those among us who had to face the daily grind just to scrape by. There were times that even I, as a middle-class educated black man, tended to forget that I grew up in the cotton and soybean fields of northeast Louisiana. I attribute that to my semi-insulation from that life because of my father's position in the community. His being a school principal shielded my siblings and me from having to perform at menial but back-breaking labor.

But Vasquez served as a constant reminder that the American Dream is there for us only if we wrest it from those who would deny us. Whether we want to admit it or not, the odds are stacked against those who are not born to privilege. Vasquez had spat in the face of those odds and had become his own man. Accordingly, I couldn't help feeling that in his own way, he was probably the most reliable—and dedicated—member of our entire team.

Still, there was no way to gauge the anxiety that gripped each person. No one has ever come up with any kind of medical device to measure raw emotions or to predict how a human being will react in a given situation. The only way to find out is to insert that person into the situation and hope for the best. Training and regimen helps, but there is no substitute for being in the real-time environment.

The best indication that everyone was holding up under the most intense pressure imaginable was the fact that there had been no defections and no leaks. Or so they thought.

40

Americans take a lot of self-pride in the myth that they live in the most democratic nation on earth. It is free and a land of opportunity to those with means and status. In the years following World War II, the American middle class prospered as never before but it did so at the expense of those without the means to purchase new cars, washing machines, refrigerators, and modern homes. Even though Barry Goldwater was swamped in the nineteen sixty-four presidential election, he laid the groundwork for Nixon's Southern Strategy and the Lewis Powell memo of 1971, alternately dubbed the *Powell Manifesto*, laid out a strategy for the conservative takeover of the government of the United States by corporate America. Powell's doctrine, written for a friend who headed the U.S. Chamber of Commerce, was largely responsible for the creation of the arch-conservative Heritage Foundation, the Manhattan Institute, and the Cato Institute, among others. Fast on the heels of those came the conservative radio and television talk show hosts who continued to feed the propaganda that everyone in America can succeed if they only get up off their collective asses and apply themselves.

All those factors, in turn, led to a transformation of the South as more and more of its politicians switched parties and to business-oriented legislation at the sacrifice of organized labor. It was organized labor that had built the nation's infrastructure and manufacturing base. But as labor was gutted in favor of the so-called right to work legislation, business and industry saw its bottom line grow exponentially. With that came heretofore unimaginable profits for stockholders and board members and obscene salaries for top corporate executives—even as wages of rank-and-file employees became more and more stagnant.

An easily discernable gulf between the haves and have-nots grew wider and wider—just as the Powell memo had laid it all out. Cooperative politicians were being propped up by the U.S. Chamber, the American Legislative Exchange Council and their propaganda machines in the conservative media. Conservative journalists and talk show hosts kept churning out stories designed to engender racial hatred, contempt for the so-called "welfare queens" who gamed the system. It didn't seem to matter that the billions of dollars stolen by Wall Street banks and hedge funds, pharmaceutical firms, energy companies, and politicians themselves far outstripped anything welfare cheats could amass. The working poor who could not afford health insurance and who had no voice to speak for them—Islamics, gays, blacks and illegal immigrants—became more and more marginalized with each passing day. Even poor whites, ironically the core of the conservative constituency, fell farther and farther behind in their efforts to capture the American dream.

It was not enough, apparently, that these tactics worked to keep a majority in Congress who could perpetuate the myth that everyone had the same opportunity but with greed, there is never enough for those who reap the bountiful goodness of a system rigged for their benefit. There has to be more to be had. As if ordained to do so, Blount stepped into the breach to announce his candidacy from his New York corporate offices. On the campaign trail, throngs of worshipers knelt at the altar of Blount, frothing at the mouth as they did so over his promises to rid the country of all evil, i.e. illegal immigrants, Islamics, and environmental regulations he proclaimed were stifling the economy.

They cut loose with rowdy rebel yells as he called out for investigations of his opponent, promised a clampdown on voter fraud and they cheered as no sports fanatic ever could when he encouraged the faithful to beat the living hell out of the occasional brave heckler at his rallies.

It was the presidential campaign that made America a laughing-stock among its enemies and which caused great concern among her allies. No one knew how to take this antithesis to the conventional politician who, in stark contrast to Blount, weighed his words carefully before responding to questions of policy. Blount never did. He would say, much to the horror of his staff, whatever popped into his mind at the moment. An hour later, his answer to the same question might be exactly the opposite to what he'd said earlier. There was no barometer, no mute button, and contrary to conventional wisdom that his mouth would eventually do him in, every utterance seemed to give only encouragement to the very low-income, trailer park constituency he and his colleagues in Congress intended to keep in their place.

They loved every hate-mongering phrase that escaped his lips and they hung on to every addle-brained idea he tossed out, including nuking America's enemies, passing stricter laws designed to imprison more minor offenders and ramping up capital punishment. Even his tax reform promises were dipped in ink designed to give the rich like himself even more tax breaks but his idolizers could not have cared less: if he said it, it was all good.

It was a society turned upside down and it was on this wave of hysteria that Blount, defying all the experts, rode into the White House. Everything would be okay now, his base told itself. Blount was going to round up all the homeless derelicts and put them in work camps. He never made such a promise but it didn't matter; that was what his supporters interpreted. Drug pushers were going down, crime was going to evaporate, and everyone was going to have a great-paying job as Blount brought overseas businesses back to the good old U.S. of A.

Illegal immigrants would be shown the door even though no one gave the first thought as to who would replace them as roofers, carpenters, painters, and other general laborers. Blacks would have to go to work and get off welfare and maybe, just maybe, Blount would clean up the voter rolls so that the Blacks wouldn't be able to vote three or four times in each election. That is what he said, wasn't it? Well, yes, but he never offered a shred of evidence as to how that would be accomplished when asked by reporters. But it didn't matter. He said it, so it must be true.

In reality, mergers would be allowed in defiance of monopolistic practices designed to drive consumer prices upward. More and more tax shelters would be created for the very rich while the middle was expected to be content with a few extra cents added to paychecks. Predictably, the strategy worked. And while no one was paying attention, Blount's appointees, political lackeys one and all, would rape agency coffers with first-class airline trips abroad, expensive office furnishings and obscene pay raises for political cronies hired on as assistants, deputies and under-secretaries. Professional staffers would be exploited as errand runners for the new-installed agency heads.

183

And the masses celebrated.

That was the unforeseen mindset that swept Blount into office with a majority of the electoral vote but with a minority of the popular vote. No one could have anticipated he would survive his party's primaries, let alone win the election. It was a fluke in every sense of the word, but Blount took it all in as a mandate and rather than being a gracious victor, he taunted the opposition to the orgasmic delight of his supporters.

In one fleeting television interview, a late-night talk show host took to conducting man-in-the-street interviews, pioneered by Art Linkletter when he was a radio personality very early in his career in San Diego. But these interviews by the number-one network talk show host, Rick Turnbow, were conducted to make a point. Turnbow, trailed by a cameraman and a grip, a crew member who held a boom microphone, would walk down a busy sidewalk seeking out Blount supporters.

The interview format was rather simple. Turnbow would ask the Blount supporter why he or she liked Blount. The typical answer would be something on the order of, "He's trying to do what he said he'd do but Congress won't let him," or "He's trying to change the way things are run in Washington," or even, "He's not a politician, he's one of us." The studio audience would break into sustained laughter at the "He's one of us" claim, as if a narcissist billionaire from New York could ever empathize with Middle America.

Turnbow would pause long enough to let the answers sink in with his audience before he would respond with six basic questions that any high school civics student should know by rote:
- How many Supreme Court justices are there?
- Can you name the two chambers of Congress?
- How many members are in the House and Senate—individually and combined?
- What are the three branches of government?
- Who are your senators?
- Who is your representative?

Invariably, he would get nothing but blank stares in response to each question. In none of his interviews did his subject know the answer to more than one or two of the queries. Of course, the interviews were cherry picked to illustrate only the general lack of knowledge about the federal government. Those who happened to know the answers never saw air time, but they were so few in number that it would have served only to underscore Turnbow's point.

His audiences, both in the studio and those watching at home loved it, but he was preaching to the choir. The ones who should have been embarrassed at the general ignorance of Americans about their government didn't watch "that liberal crap" anyway. So, those who comprised Blount's base continued to go about their daily lives secure in the knowledge that he was doing all in his power to restore the American Dream.

There were two Americas, not only in economic terms but philosophically, as well, and the divide was widening with each passing day.

That and a seemingly unrelated but fateful NASA mission into a heretofore unexplored corner of space, combined with a growing sense of despair among mental health professionals, propelled the formulation of two independent plans involving three separate cartels divided into at least eight teams to take this man down before he could inflict irreparable damage to an already troubled, war-scarred world.

It was into this breach that Whitten and the rest threw themselves.

41

There was always the slim chance that some of us would come away from this awful exploit unscathed, so nothing was committed to writing. Throwaway cell phones were used in lieu of landlines or our regular cellular instruments. Each member of the cabal had standing instructions to destroy and replace existing the throwaway instruments weekly and to let the other members know the new numbers.

New phones were never purchased from the same source as any previous one. Often the purchaser would travel completely across Houston—or even to Vidor or Beaumont or The Woodlands to get a new phone. It was a complicated but vitally necessary precautionary measure designed to conceal any link to each other from prying eyes. Times and locations of meetings changed on a regular basis so as not to establish any discernable pattern. Even different modes of transportation were used to get to the meeting sites. Sometimes personal vehicles were used. Other times, Uber and taxi services were employed and sometimes even mass transit, bicycles and motorcycles were chosen. At one meeting, one of our select group showed up sweating and panting—in running shorts.

If you've ever experienced any degree of paranoia, then you may have some idea—but only an inkling—of the extent of our obsession with secrecy. At the same time, each of us was trying our best to carry on a normal home life, interacting with family and friends as if life was sedate and wonderful, which, of course, it most certainly was not. There was not one of the seven of us who were not living on the ragged edge that consisted of a steady diet of antacids, sleepless nights, and feigned calm. Now, as we deployed for our respective destinations, each knowing that he or she could be the one to carry out the ultimate objective, those feelings were intensified by a factor we could not begin to calculate. Twenty-four/seven heartburn was now the norm.

42

When Secretary of Housing and Urban Development Scott Rankin and Secretary of Health and Human Services Alexander Goulart, at Blount's direction, began implementing the president's orders to increase rent threefold for federally-subsidized housing and simultaneously separating adolescent children from their illegal immigrant parents and slashing programs like Meals-on-Wheels and heating fuel assistance, the mood of the nation immediately grew dark and ugly.

It was one thing to remove key restrictions on the banking and hedge fund industries, restrictions that reined in reckless investing of customer's retirement funds. Even Blount's silly, ill-advised diplomatic bluster and his embracing of international tyrants couldn't seem to shake his core support. Nor did his refusal to condemn racist rhetoric at right-wing rallies on university campuses or even in Washington, D.C. And his refusal to endorse stricter background checks on weapons purchases in the wake of mass shootings across the national landscape couldn't make a dent in his solid thirty-five to forty percent support.

But it was quite another thing for Americans to have images beamed into their living rooms on the nightly news of elderly shut-ins going hungry for a lack of food while bundled in layers of blankets because they could not afford fuel to keep their houses warm. For the first time, his polling numbers began to look shaky when television cameras revealed graphic images of meager belongings piled on curbsides as low-income, mostly minority families, many of them headed by single mothers, were evicted from federally-subsidized housing because they could no longer afford their rent which had trebled literally overnight.

And those poll numbers plunged even further as America was

shamed into watching screaming, traumatized pre-school children desperately crying out for their mommies and daddies as they were herded into improvised chain link cages in deserted box stores. Meanwhile, their parents, who had fled from despots of their Latin American countries sought asylum in the one country where they thought they might find refuge, were transported a thousand miles away with no way to contact their children. As congressmen were turned away from the holding centers, American's frustration grew. *If a congressman can't make his voice heard, how can we?*

The evictions, cessation of services for the elderly shut-ins, and the inhumane treatment of little children put a human face on the depth of cruelty to which Blount was showing he could stoop. It was as if Americans were confronting their own callousness and indifference to human suffering—and indeed, they were. And the people were uncomfortable with the images of themselves that they were being forced to watch.

The president's approval rating dropped precipitously to seventeen percent, the lowest of any president since such polls had been taken. By comparison, Nixon was a shining beacon of care and compassion. The numbers threatened to go even lower.

Blount's answer to this public relations disaster was to schedule a weekend of golf.

43

Booth and I checked into a Marriot near Blount's golf club. We took separate rooms and we were careful not to be seen together. I could immediately feel the walls closing in on me in my room. I tried to watch television but could think of nothing but the mission and Phoebe back home. It was a strange emptiness as I contemplated the prospect of killing a man I'd never met who just happened to be the most powerful man on the face of the earth all the while of knowing I would very likely never see my family again. That the world was blissfully ignorant of what lay in store for the entire planet if the mission was not carried out only served to remind me of the disgrace I was about to bring on my family's name. This did nothing to assuage my burden.

As fate would have it, the newscast on CNN caught my attention when it was announced that Blount would indeed appear at the ARMS convention. With a crowd of ten thousand on hand to cheer his rhetoric, it was too good an opportunity for him to pass up. He would speak there and then retire to his local resort for a weekend of golf. The CNN announcer reported in a voice-over report as video showed Blount boarding a Marine helicopter to transport him to Air Force One which would fly him in all the creature comforts imaginable to South Florida. As pre-determined, Booth would be at the ARMS convention and I would stake out the golf course—the two of us far enough from Secret Service details to avoid detection but close enough for our weapons to be effective.

Sleep, of course, was impossible. I don't know what Booth was doing during the night which seemed to last forever and to fly by at the same time, but I know I wept and I prayed. And then I threw up again. At dawn, I caught the elevator down to the hotel lobby for a continental breakfast of eggs, bacon, biscuits, orange juice, and coffee. And more coffee. I picked over the eggs and bacon and left the biscuits untouched. Food was out of the question because my stomach was churning. I managed to finish the orange juice and four cups of coffee before heading back to my room.

As I inserted the card into the door, I could hear the room phone ringing from the other side of the heavy door. No one knew where I was, not even Booth, so I had no idea who would be calling me other than perhaps hotel personnel.

Opening the door, I made it to the phone on the table between the two beds in the room in three long strides and picked up the receiver.

"Hello?"

Silence.

"Hello?"

"Colonel Whitten?"

"Who is this?" I demanded. How did this person, a voice I didn't recognize—a voice, in fact, that sounded electronically distorted.

"You don't need to know my identity," he answered. This time I could tell for certain that the voice was distorted. I felt ice surge through my veins as a cold fear enveloped my very being. I knew in an instant our security had been breached. But by whom? And how much did they know?

"You are to stand down immediately. Is that understood?"

A dry knot the size of a grapefruit made its way from my throat into my mouth and it took every ounce of determination for me to ask, "Stand down from what? Who are you?" My voice sounded detached from my being, as if the words were originating from elsewhere but somehow projected through my mouth and lips in an odd croak.

"I told you. You don't need to know who I am. Just know that your entire operation has been compromised and you are to stand down. Your entire team is being closely monitored."

"I don't know what the hell you're talking about. Is this some kind of joke?" I was trying to sound confident but I wasn't even convincing myself as I peeked through the curtains in search of the black SUVs I was certain would come screeching into the hotel parking lot any second. Three floors below, on the parking lot, all was normal. No black SUVs.

"We mean you no harm and no one will ever learn of your intent. But the matter is in better hands. There are forces at play here that you do not understand—that you don't *want* to understand. This is being taken care by professionals who know what they're doing and who, though appreciative, do not require your assistance. Just know that you're in way over your head, so you are commanded to stand down."

I groped for something to say but could come up with nothing. Finally, he continued.

"Go home to your family and have a good life, sir."

The line went dead. I looked down at my hands. They were shaking uncontrollably. If I were to have tried to shave at that point, I most probably would've cut my throat. I was still holding the hotel phone receiver in my hand when my throw away cell phone buzzed. It was Booth.

"I know I'm not supposed to contact you, but did you just get a call on the hotel phone?"

"You, too?" I stammered.

"Colonel, what the hell's going on?" He blurted. "Who were they and how did they know?"

I tried to think of an answer but I couldn't. Finally, I said, "I don't know who that was, what they know or how they know. But I do know one thing: we have a job to do and we're not about to let a bunch of spooks prevent us from carrying out our mission. We knew the dangers going in. Nothing's changed."

"Yes, sir," he said.

"Now destroy your phone and I'll do the same and we won't contact each other again, got it?"

"Affirmative."

I disconnected the call and walked to the door of my room. Easing the door open a couple of inches, I looked up and down the hallway and, seeing no one, slipped the phone into the opening and pushed the door tight onto the instrument. I then threw my entire weight into the door, crushing the instrument. I picked up the pieces to be discarded when I was far away from the hotel. I quickly went about getting dressed to leave for Blount's resort golf club. Then I saw the bulletin from CNN flash onto the television screen not six feet from where I was standing:

"PRESIDENT BLOUNT STRICKEN, RUSHED TO HOSPITAL. CONDITION UNKNOWN."

In my heart of hearts, I knew the news bulletin and the cryptic phone calls Booth and I received moments before were related. I sank onto the side of the bed because my knees could no longer support my body. I also knew what no other person on earth other than Booth and those individuals who had carried out the actual deed: that Blount was already dead or dying. A combined wave of foreboding, uncertainty, shock—and an incredible rush of relief—swept over my very soul at once. There is no way to begin to describe the range of emotions I experienced in the moments immediately following the call and the news bulletin.

I wanted more than anything else the one thing that I dare not trust myself to do.

I wanted to call Phoebe and tell her I loved her and the kids. But I knew I'd lose it. I lost it anyway.

I managed to lie back on the bed and stare at the ceiling, hoping that I might somehow stop the shaking and the sobbing that were wracking my body

44

The Youngs, Nathan and Jonathan, and their Terranumite team members in Florida, Texas and New Jersey, all saw the news bulletins as well. Two of the teams were in Texas and New Jersey and were preparing for their next assignment now that they knew Blount was not in either of those states for the weekend. Bob Hastings, the one who had trained the Terranumites, was one of those in Texas. Two others, like Booth and I, were in Florida, their weapons cleaned and ready for their assignment until they, like the two of us, had received orders from a disembodied voice via a hotel switchboard, effectively concealing the caller's identity, instructing them to abort their mission. As was the case with us, they had decided to ignore their mysterious instructions—until they heard the news of Blount's sudden illness.

Nguyen Huy, cloistered in Santa Barbara, Sarah Bergmann in San Antonio, Dr. Hubballi Patel in Atlantic City, Colonel Damon Wilhite in Houston, Rafael Vasquez and his fellow Terranumites in the same locations as well as another team in Washington were passing the time in their rooms or standing around in airport terminals awaiting their flights home when the news hit. As expected, everyone assumed that someone affiliated with their group may have been successful in carrying out the hit. Everything had been so well-planned, after all. They were incorrect. Now they sat staring at unblinking TV monitors to hear the latest update on Blount's conditions. Only Booth and I, along with the two unknown Terranumites also in South Florida found any updates unnecessary. We all knew without being told what the next announcement would be and we knew it wouldn't be made until it was certain that the Vice President was safe and ready to be sworn in.

At 11:18 a.m. Eastern Time, the official word went out. Blount was dead. The cause of his sudden death was not immediately available. Translated: the official cover-up had begun.

Huy and Patel were already in airports in Los Angeles and Newark. It was only 8:18 in California. Audible cries escaped the throats of passengers moving to and from flights in both cities as crowds around the TV monitors grew into the thousands in what seemed to be only seconds. In Newark, one person clapped and another cheered and instantly, the crowd was embroiled in a free-for-all and security had to be called in to break up the fighting.

Across the country, traffic came to a standstill, businesses closed either in celebration or mourning. There was no consensus as to whether Blount's death was a tragedy or a national blessing. One thing was for certain, however: no one was neutral.

A great wave of relief quietly encircled the globe as leaders in international capitals in Canada, Central and South America, Asia, Europe and Africa whispered a silent prayer of thanks for divine intervention on behalf of world peace, such as it was, while publicly expressing their deep and sincere condolences to the American people and to the President's family. It was all a sham and everyone in Washington knew it but everyone agreed—publicly. It was a terrible loss to the U.S. and to the world. They agreed with the sentiments being expressed even while vowing to themselves that the country and the world must never be brought to a point this near the precipice of destruction ever again.

45

The right-wing extremist blogs wasted no time regurgitating their conspiracy theories. The imagined plots offered up by the JFK assassination buffs paled by comparison. Where they generally limited their perpetrators to Castro, the mob or the Teamsters, the newest wave of renderings, given even wider circulation via the Internet, were all over the map. Suspects included minority leaders in Congress, the former President who happened to be African-American, Islamics, illegal immigrants from Latin America, and even the media itself, in search of a new lead story on a slow news day Saturday.

About the only ones never mentioned as potential suspects in the countless, non-stop blog posts were members of NASA, psychiatrists, or Terranumites. Nor were they ever mentioned in any official documents concerning Blount's untimely demise, though there were plenty of those to go around.

There was one arrest. An employee who worked in the kitchen of Blount's resort hotel, was "apprehended" and secreted off to Guantanamo. The reasons given alluded to the suspect's safety but the real reason, of course, was that he would be out of reach to an inquiring media. After a respectable period of time, enough time for an "official inquiry" to be conducted, the National Security Administration, chosen because of the lofty implications that went with its name, issued its report.

It intoned in the most clinical of terms that Novichok, the same Russian-made nerve agent employed in the poisoning of Russian double agent Sergei Skripal and his daughter Yulia in March of 2018, was the means by which Blount died. Novichok, administered in large dosages, attacks the respiratory muscles and the central nervous systems, causing its victim to suffocate. Highly concentrated traces of the nerve agent were found on Blount's silverware, his water glass and his coffee cup. They were all on his breakfast tray that had been delivered to his hotel room the morning of his death. The report noted that the tray was prepared by kitchen employee Julio Martinez, whose wife and children had been deported as part of Blount's crackdown on illegal immigration. It omitted, however, the key fact that the tray had been delivered to Blount's room by a Secret Service agent who had suddenly—and conveniently—disappeared. Apparently, it never occurred to anyone in authority to look for the agent since they had their man in the person of Martinez. And Martinez would die within a week when it was said he attempted to escape by grabbing a guard's weapon and was cut down in a hail of gunfire. At least, that was the official word—and there were no witnesses to challenge the story.

A blue-ribbon commission was appointed to take testimony, to study evidence and to issue a final report on Blount's death—which would be anything *but* final with all the speculation being fanned by conspiracy fanatics. The fact that the commission consisted of members of Congress, the Supreme Court and other Washington officials only heightened the distrust of its findings even before they were released. Even those who never clicked onto the wild-eyed bloggers' links were convinced that the report would be a fictionalized accounting of the facts, a varnished version of the truth done to protect Americans from themselves. They were correct, of course. And, predictably, much of the testimony gleaned for the report would be sealed for seventy-five years.

First of all, the final report, released seven months after Blount's death, said, Martinez had acted alone. There was no evidence of a conspiracy, it said. Whitten and the others were incredulous that such a brazen assessment could be made by serious men and women when all the evidence already known indicated otherwise. Not addressed was how Martinez would have been able to access the nerve agent that was manufactured in Russia and nowhere else. Only someone either affiliated closely with the Russians or who worked in the upper reaches of U.S. intelligence would be able to obtain the agent. Also not addressed was how Martinez would have been able to get the tray to Blount without either exposing himself or being discovered. Was the tray contaminated when it left the kitchen or was the nerve agent administered somewhere between the kitchen and Blount's room. Nowhere in the commission's report was that discussed. And what of the Secret Service agent who simply vanished? He was never mentioned and the American citizens never knew of his existence. Only a small circle of top-secret personnel knew about him. And they weren't talking.

The blogosphere went ballistic. The report was ripped by the right-wing extremists, by the leftwing radicals and by the moderates in between. No one was buying its official version. Yet, it stood. A cloak of secrecy spread over the Beltway, covering the truth and silencing the protests the way a thick blanket of snow covers the landscape and muffles out the sounds of everyday noise.

Dr. Frederick Feinberg and his Association of Patriotic Psychiatrists disappeared from view for an extended time, never having ever been a real factor in the rush of events that transpired in those hectic final days. APP's attack ads calling Blount's mental capabilities into question were instantly turned on the organization and its credibility evaporated overnight as public opinion went from general indifference before the President's death to outright hostility afterwards.

Feinberg, because of the exploitation of his profession as a means of opposing Blount, became an unfortunate victim of circumstances. He began running into ethical problems from psychiatric regulatory boards, eventually losing his practice and his license. He was forced to resort to contracting his services out as a psychiatric expert for criminal defense attorneys. Time after time, he would be subjected to withering humiliation at the hands of merciless prosecuting attorneys who never failed to call attention to his history as leader of APP.

46

Disillusionment can take on many forms. Too often, we elevate men and women to hero status when in the end they are merely men and women who, like us, strive only to survive in a world gone mad. Scoring touchdowns or hitting home runs or making great speeches can turn the spotlight of idolization on them momentarily but even that burns out quickly in relation to time. If you don't believe that, try asking a kid who Henry Aaron or Bob Gibson are. Ask an adult about Eisenhower's warning about the influence of the military-industrial complex or about Charles Lindbergh's stance on America's entry into World War II. Ask anyone you meet on the street to tell you about Seward's Folly. We place people like John Wayne, on a pedestal. Wayne made about a dozen war movies but never served a day in the military. A third of Louisiana Republicans polled in 2013 blamed Barack Obama for the federal government's pitifully slow response to Hurricane Katrina in 2005. Obama did not become president until 2008.

Others, like Thomas Jefferson and Andrew Jackson, take on larger-than-life roles. Jefferson, of course, wrote the Declaration of Independence and Jackson defeated British General Sir Edward Pakenham at the Battle of New Orleans, albeit after the treaty was signed ending the War of 1812. That made them genuine heroes to me when I was growing up in the Louisiana Delta. Only later would I learn of the atrocities committed against the Native Americans by Jackson or the slave woman that Jefferson impregnated while proclaiming more than a little hypocritically that all people are created equal.

The greatness of America, a greatness I had been taught from childhood, was tarnished. I would learn in my adulthood, by the concept of Manifest Destiny, the idea that the white man was entitled to land held by the red man. The Monroe Doctrine only served to further embolden the encroachment upon Native Americans. And of America's heroic wars, I learned the heroism was largely manufactured. The Mexican War only served as a means for the U.S. to rip about a third of Mexico's land from her, including almost all of present-day New Mexico, Nevada, Utah, California, and Arizona. And American leaders to this day continue to rant about illegal immigrants pouring into the U.S. from our southern border. Native might have something to say about that themselves—if only they had a voice to speak on their behalf.

In Mississippi, Alabama, and in Louisiana where I grew up, grown men still fly the Confederate flag from the backs of their pickup trucks in apparent homage to a concept that certain people were endowed with the right to enslave certain other people. The irony of that is that the ancestors of those flying the flags were most probably not the ones who held that right until it was taken away only to be replaced by something called convict leasing, which in reality, was just another form of slavery, but legal. Their ancestors were quite likely the poor white trash of their day, an irony lost on the latter-day defenders of the so-called southern legacy.

And as probably the best example of all, we had something called the Vietnam War to look to. In that war, in which more than three million Asians died in a struggle for independence from French colonialism, there was Lieutenant William Calley, who led the massacre of Vietnamese civilians at My Lai until Warrant Officer Hugh Thompson intervened by landing his helicopter between Calley's men and the Vietnamese. Instead of recognizing Thompson's heroics in halting the wholesale slaughter as it should have, the Army attempted to cover up the entire event and make Calley the hero instead.

Which is very much what happened in Blount's case. I knew, and my team and the Terranumites knew, that Martinez, if involved at all, surely did not act alone. Blount's death, was part of an intricate plot, as evidenced by at least three secretive telephone calls from unidentified callers in positions to make the crucial calls to The Terranumite team, to Booth and to me. The hit was carried out by highly-placed insiders within the Blount administration. One of them told me it was being taken care of only minutes before the news first hit CNN. That had to mean the execution was already underway as we were speaking.

Somewhere in the nation's capital or maybe in America's heartland, someone with a lot of power and influence, and doubtless, a lot of money, who possesses tremendous leverage over the lives of millions of people, knows the true story of the death of President Andrus Blount. That someone is still pulling the levers of government—good or bad—and they're still expressing their profound grief at the tragic assassination of such a strong leader by some lone dissident, a man deeply embittered at the deportation of his family.

After Blount's death, we never saw each other again. The crew of Sol Orbiter One never set foot on another space shuttle. We resigned from NASA en masse, no explanations given, none asked. Each of us has gone our separate ways, embarking on new careers. No contact was ever attempted with any of the Terranumites we met during our secret mission. I don't know what ever became of Vasquez, the Terranumite member of our Sol Orbiter One crew, but I would hazard a guess that he succeeded in whatever endeavor he attempted.

But I do know one thing with absolute certainty. None of us—Terranumites nor members of the historic Sol Orbiter One mission—will ever look upon our government, our elected leaders, in the same light again.

There is just something about betrayal and duplicity that stays with you forever and it won't let go no matter how hard you try. We thought that with Hitler but someone once said that history is doomed to repeat itself.

You'd think our political leaders would eventually learn that important lesson.

But then, I guess not.